CONFUSED BASTARDS

CONFUSED BASTARDS

Manav Vigg

Srishti
Publishers & Distributors

Srishti Publishers & Distributors
Registered Office: N-16, C.R. Park
New Delhi – 110 019
Corporate Office: 212A, Peacock Lane
Shahpur Jat, New Delhi – 110 049
editorial@srishtipublishers.com

First published by
Srishti Publishers & Distributors in 2016

10 9 8 7 6 5 4 3 2 1

Printed and bound in India

Gratitude

The Big Bang*

*Only if it actually happened!

Acknowledgements

This is my first story and it couldn't have been possible without the support of some people. I want to take this opportunity to thank them for their presence in my life.

1. **Shobha Nihalani** (shobhanihalani@gmail.com), Editor – Thank you Shobha for believing in my story and my style of writing when no one else did. You gave me confidence and relentless support, and offered to edit the novel. Thanks to your guidance and strength, this story is finally reaching people.
2. **Gaurav Sahni** for taking the initiative to take this story to people. Your unconditional support and positive energy made this journey possible.
3. **My family** – my parents for letting me take the leap when I needed it the most; my sister and my brother-in-law for being my pillars of strength and humour; my beautiful niece for giving us a new lease of life when she blessed us with her presence last year.
4. **My Friends -** Ruchi Sahni, Ayush Anand, Ashutosh Kaushik, Dhiraj Gupta, Ashutosh Matela, Utkarsh Arora, Anurag Kapoor, Pranav Mahadevia and Sudhir Bhoj for having faith in me.
5. **My publisher** – For your faith in my work when it mattered the most; the entire editorial team of Srishti for making the novel really crisp and flowing.
6. **Kanupriya Gupta** – My cover designer, for brainstorming for several months before arriving at this unique and beautiful book cover.

And last, but never the least, my readers. I eagerly look forward to hearing from you. You can send in your thoughts and observations at confusedbastards@gmail.com.

Prologue

?

Aakash, Jai and Vivek, three wannabe achievers, were led by Sattu to the large terrace of his luxurious three-storey house. The terrace was vast enough to hold three mandaps, if they all chose to get married at the same time. But this was not the time to get hitched. This was the time to focus on where they were being led – a promised dream. In the corner of the terrace, there was a green glass shed. Inside, a servant was spreading a pile of dried leaves on a table while the other assistant stood next to a table fan. The sun's rays penetrating through the glass made the lighting appropriate for the camera set up on a tripod.

Jai and Vivek exchanged knowing glances. This was a macho Aakash moment. He strode in with his chest puffed out, his moustached face facing the camera. His six-foot frame and sturdy body was perfect hero material. Feet shoulder-width apart, he stood at the position marked on the floor and faced the camera with an air of confidence. Sattu panned Aakash from head to shoulders. He then gestured for the table fan to be switched on. The pile of leaves began to stir while Aakash was poised to speak.

"Aaaaaaaccttiiooonn!" declared Sattu.

His hero began with controlled confidence.

"Hi! My name is Aakash Srivastava, son of an IAS officer. I was born in Delhi, brought up in several cities of India. Schooled in science, my graduation was in humanities and my MBA in Marketing. I started my first business soon after, when I partnered with some friends and launched a website. It didn't succeed, so I switched to the restaurant business in South Delhi, which again didn't click. I didn't lose hope and soon after that, ventured to my third business in engineering education. Ha! And what a useless effort! I forgot that there are more engineers than donkeys in this country. Then I explored a website business by the name www.ihafa.in which did well, but didn't last."

He took a deep breath.

"For all you aspiring men and women, this shows that the main reason for not succeeding is that I didn't persist long enough in any one business. As a result, I lost interest and the whole self-made man ideology went to pot. I think the same logic holds true when it comes to girls. I start dating a girl and immediately lose interest. But, in this fast-paced instant meal world, what else can you expect! I openly admit to being a Confused Bastard."

"That was bloody pathetic! You cannot just say it so casually," snapped Sattu. "Say it with passion so that the whole world understands what a CB you are."

"I think the whole world will be able to figure it out!"

"You better listen to me! You wanted this entire set up, the flying leaves, and all this crap simply to spill your gut and I provided all of that. Now, you have to tell the truth my style – with energy!"

Jai and Vivek exchanged glances. It was a battle of wills and egos. Not that their glances remained serious for long. But this time they were concerned. As if reading Sattu's mind and what his 'style' entailed, Aakash's face turned red and his jaw worked with repressed anger. He retreated to his position and started his oration.

"My name is Aakash Srivastava. Look at me. Look at me all you mother fucking people living on this crazy planet. I have never stuck to one business or girl in my entire miserable life. But I was not like that. As a child, I used to be extremely focussed. But two major events made me the way I am today – puberty and globalization. And both those fucking events gave me endless possibilities in business and sex. And today, facing this fucking camera is a guy who does not know what to do with his life and whom to fuck. In a nutshell, I declare that I am a Confused Bastard!"

They all clapped thunderously. Sattu's face was filled with pride as if he had achieved his life's purpose.

"Brilliant!"

The video was ready to be uploaded onto today's version of Sanjay's Divya Chakshu used for narration of the war of Mahabharata – YouTube.

Dark Night Crisis

?

Before the sun appeared and the rooster announced its wake-up call, Vivek had taken the pledge of bathing with the deities every morning. This didn't upset the Sun, the rooster, or the deities, but it definitely upset Jai and Aakash. While they slept the peaceful sleep of the dead, sprawled across their beds, their intoxicated minds spinning lazily over wet dreams, they could not escape the sounds of Vivek's chanting. His tuneless voice was stereophonically enhanced with the rooster announcing the dawn of a brand new day.

"Om namah Shivaye...Om namah Shivaye...Om namah Shivaye!"

Vivek's voice was a loud tremor as he began his morning bath routine. Hands stretched above his head, he poured the ice-cold water over the strands of thinning hair on his otherwise bald dome. The water slid down his bearded face, made its way over his lean dusky physique of a little above five feet. His feeble voice quivered during the waterfall which he kept up at regular intervals. *"Jai Hanuman gyan gun sagar!"*

Vivek made his way to another deity, his tremulous voice was even louder and the rooster competed eagerly with Vivek's energetic vibrato.

Aakash and Jai muttered in their sleep, still immersed in a world of illusions.

"Hello *kaun? Meri Maa*...Jai Hooo!"

Now that was louder than a train's siren, which ruined his friends' dreams.

The word 'Maa' had a magical effect on Jai. He turned on his side and sighed. "I am hungry". The rooster's crowing stretched echoing deeply, and the sun finally managed to dodge the dark clouds sending out rays of hope.

Vivek wasted the last bucket of water in his attempt to wake the Gods:

"Jo bole so nihaal, Sat Shri Akaal!"

Aakash and Jai snapped awake, uttering abuse at their roommate. Aakash repeated, *"Fuck you asshole"* and Jai repeated his routine line – *"Doob ja saale usi paani mein...din mein Boss nahi sone deta aur raat ko ye pakhandi."* Both sank back into their pillows. The cock was terrified by the human voices and went mute. And as if on cue, darkness descended as the clouds returned.

Vivek came out of the bathroom in his dhoti. Seeming unperturbed by his friends' comments, he lit an agarbatti and placed it inside a small prayer shelf, suspended from one of the walls of his room. This quintessential stuffy bachelor home which otherwise reeked of alcohol, didn't affect his spiritual endeavors. The infusion of aggarbati and alcohol gave him the perfect balance to ponder over his dilemma in this material world and his spiritual life.

•

The sun shone fearlessly. There was a morning bustle as people got ready for the day, but Aakash and Jai were still in their intoxicated sleep.

Jai suddenly woke up with a bad feeling in his gut – must be the beer and overindulgence of chicken tikkas. With an average height of five feet six inches and a chubby Punjabi physique, he was the stereotypical fair and lovely North Indian with a round face.

Jai checked the watch on his bedside table. It was 8 a.m. Given the fact that he needed to be in his office at Gurgaon by nine, and his travelling time from Delhi city was about an hour, he needed to decide which morning chore to skip. In split-second, he went through his list:

Shitting: Given his boss's personality, he would in any case shit in his pants, so may as well save it for the office.

Shaving: He was relieved from that duty. He had been praying to God since puberty to give him some facial hair.

Bathing: Well, this was a weekly activity and not necessary considering the range of deodorants available in the market. He may as well fog himself.

Brushing: He noticed a packet of Chiclets next to the alarm clock. Good enough.

By this time, Vivek had graduated to yoga poses and started with his breathing exercises. He followed the audio instructions streaming from his mobile phone. At the same time, Jai dashed speedily, searching for clothes and shoes. This was their routine of synchronized huffing and puffing – Vivek seated and Jai stressing.

As Vivek continued with the yoga instructions, he discerned a different voice humming along in an orgasmic fashion:

"Ek naak se ander lijiye aur doosri se chhodiye...ab doosri se ander lijiye aur pehli se chhodiye...ab dono se ander lijiye."

Vivek opened his eyes to see Aakash standing in front of him. With a height of over six feet and a well-toned physique, Vivek strained his neck to look up at Aakash's sturdy face. And even though Aakash's red-rimmed eyes were evidence of troubled sleep, he managed to maintain a smirk.

Jai had made it to undies and an unbuttoned shirt.

"Sorry...can I borrow your trousers?" he squeaked.

Vivek ignored his semi-nude friend and confronted the recently awakened zombie. "You have this bad habit of disturbing my peace! Can you please leave me alone?"

"Just for today!" called out Jai.

"Just for today," stated Vivek, eyes on Aakash.

"It's very urgent!" insisted Jai, looking at his two friends eyeing each other like predators.

"It's very urgent," continued Vivek in a monotone.

"I promise I won't ask for anything else," Jai added desperately.

"I promise I won't ask for anything else." Vivek seemed in a hypnotic state.

The sarcastic repetition irked Jai. "Hey assholes, I'm getting late!"

Vivek was shaken out of his reverie and looked irritated. "Why do you have to ask the same thing every day? Go take my trousers and get lost!" Jai grabbed the trousers and put them on.

"Why are you up so early?" Vivek vented at Aakash who normally woke up close to noon.

"That joker disturbed me. Why the fuck does he even go to office?" demanded Aakash putting the blame on his friend, an employee with a mobile company. Jai shook his head.

"You are not helping," replied Vivek who wanted to continue with his yoga.

"I am helping you baby. *Ek naak se ander lo aur doosre se chhod do.*"

Vivek realized there was no point arguing. He got up and went to the kitchen to make coffee. Jai was about to exit only to be stopped by Aakash.

"Hey fucker...listen up!"

"Now what?"

"Do you know how many days you are going to survive this ass-biting job of yours?"

"What diff to you?"

"Because my dear friend, the telecom sector is fucked...the margins are extinct with the dinosaurs."

"So what? It's not my dad's company."

"Exactly! That's what I call employee mentality. Just change the job!"

Vivek returned with the coffee and gestured to Jai to leave, who gladly obliged. Vivek and Aakash sipped their brew in silence while contemplating on life and Jai.

"Why do you screw with him?" Vivek started.

"He has got potential. Why the hell can't he sell his own products?"

"He has got none…it's not easy to create your own products."

"I will create products for him."

"Don't start off with your fantasies in the morning."

"No, seriously….I have a fantastic idea."

"You mean another plan for another goof up?"

"All great businessmen have goofed up some time or the other. I mean, look at this guy." Aakash pointed to an article in the newspaper he had just picked up.

"This bugger explored five different website businesses and finally struck gold with the last one. Sold it for a hundred crores!"

"Well fine, let's talk about something interesting. Like, how was yesterday?" Vivek replied, in no mood for discussions regarding finance.

Aakash got excited.

"Legendary! Only if someone could photoshoot me in different postures with her, I can come up with the modern day version of the *Kamasutra*." Aakash always seemed to be buzzed about two things – business and sex.

"Is she that flexible?"

"She is the epitome of flexibility. She is a dancer."

"So, you done with her?"

"Why? Do you want her? "

"No thanks."

"You still can't get over that girl?"

"Don't call her that girl," glared Vivek.

"I am sorry. Aarti. Do you really think you will be able to forget her through yoga?"

"Well, I am trying and I might if someone does not disturb me," Vivek replied.

"It's useless. If you want to forget her, get into someone else's skirt."

Vivek glanced at Aakash in irritation who continued further to pacify him. "Okay. Do it your way! The spirited way to get into someone's skirt."

Vivek nodded casually to avoid any further conversation and closed his eyes, even though his mind wandered to his marriage – the only thing in life in which he had failed.

Mogambo Khush Nahin Hua

?

The journey to the office was arduous to say the least. Jai hopped onto a bus, then a metro train ride and finally an autorickshaw to reach his workplace, which he used to cherish once upon a time. Working in the Corporate Sales division of a telecom company and getting bashed regularly for targets was not the ideal welcome. His boss, Amrit Kapoor, an early achiever, developed a sadistic pleasure in torturing his employees with abuses and taunts.

Physically, he was a six-foot bald giant who resembled Mogambo, but was never *khush*.

Jai was already late for the Friday meeting. He noticed that everyone had gathered in the conference room and the discussion had already begun. His boss was already in rant-mode, shouting at his colleagues. Well, his normal conversation always appeared animated, loud and aggressive. Jai caught some of his expletives, but for added impact, Amrit Kapoor's body language was more abusive. Jai panicked, he would rather skip the meeting, but then he would have to face the wild beast in person.

While Jai was contemplating his next move, Amrit caught sight of him and opened the door to shout, "Is there glue on your shoes?"

Jai shook his head without uttering a word.

"Then what the fuck are you doing outside? What's the bloody time?" Amrit yelled.

Jai checked his wrist and realized that he had lost his watch in a bet to Aakash. He got out his mobile phone to check the time, but it was already dead. Shit!

In a bid to avoid boss's scowling expression, his glance fell on a wall clock in the conference room.

"It's 9.20, sir," he blurted in a squeaky voice.

"You have no sense of time! Now get in here and stick your ass on that seat!" barked Amrit as Jai entered meekly and sat down. Working with Amrit felt like schooldays all over again. Amrit was the control freak, egotistic, maniac teacher/boss, who, given an option, would also want to control which way the wind blew.

"Show me your figures now!"

Jai noticed some of the heads turn up, including Sheena's, his definite well-wisher who gestured to him to go ahead. He finally spoke and revealed his figures.

"Sir, my target was one crore for the last month, and I have achieved 1.15 crores."

"That's the reason you are still in this job, you ass! What about next month?"

"I will definitely cross 1.15 crores, sir," replied Jai hoping to end his ordeal.

"No, you will cross one-and-a-half crores. That is your target for this month!"

"But sir—" A shocked Jai stared at the monster. When Jai had lost his watch in a bet to Aakash, he suffered a severe shock. He had predicted it to rain with the dark clouds, but it hadn't. But Mogambo boss was the icing on the shock cake and his demand was an unreachable target.

"What?" Amrit's voice carried an evil bent; he was ready to kill. Jai had to speak up or his ass would be up for kick sale.

"Sir...can we please revisit the target?" What courage can stupidity bring!

"Okay. Let's make it two crores!" The boss was the ultimate asshole.

"Sir, I mean can we please reduce it a bit!" Another courageous effort and he had now won a free smoke and tea from his colleagues.

Boss grinned. "Can we please reduce your salary then, sir? I mean with the pressure on margins, the company is not able to afford people who cannot generate volumes. What do you think? One-and-a-half or two crores?"

"One-and-a-half, sir!" Jai responded forcefully. This was the typical specialty of Boss Amrit. He could really hit below the belt to get his work done.

Evil Boss Amrit decided to generalize the ordeal for the room. "Guys! These are tough times and it will get tougher day by day. Competition is a bitch and we need to be like dogs to smell the bitch from far off. You all need to gear up and have balls of iron. Because if you don't, tough decisions will have to be taken. I don't need to give any further indications."

Ruining Fridays and weekends was Amrit's achievement. But like mosquitoes discovered how to survive repellants, his employees were now learning to survive him. The guy who already knew this trick was Gaurav, a colleague of Jai and Sheena's, who had now become their senior.

After the meeting, Jai joined Gaurav and Sheena for a smoke and some fresh air. They left the office and approached a chaiwaala. As they sipped hot tea and puffed on cigarettes, they could not help but discuss their targets.

"Ass, dog, bitch, balls – from where does he come up with such vocab?" fumed Sheena, sucking hard on her ciggie. "I mean, he does not even give a fuck that there are ladies in the room!"

"He believes in equality of gender!" replied Gaurav trying to lighten the mood.

"But this is going over my head now. Last year they fired two hundred people. Now they plan to fire more. What he said inside was nothing but an indication of the events to follow," remarked Jai.

"It's brutal. Last time, they didn't even spare Mishraji. He had been in the organization for over fourteen years," Sheena said. "The guy has

EMIs running, children who are in school, parents who are old and have medical expenses and he was the only earning member of his family. He is still looking for a job!"

Sheena reacted in hyper mode when it came to office politics. Attributed with a good height and an attractive body, men were attracted to her. But she knew how to tackle them. She developed what others in the office called 'you don't mess with Sheena' attitude. So if someone stared at her curves, she would give a 'you don't mess with Sheena stare'. If someone tried to play smart, she would give a 'you don't mess with Sheena finger'. If someone tried to play politics in office, she would send out a 'you don't mess with Sheena mail'. And the most dangerous of all: If someone tried to speak ill about her, she would give a 'you don't mess with Sheena confrontation'. Very few people in the organization were in her good books, and Jai was one of them.

"Relax guys. You can't expect loyalty considerations in today's world. This is the globalized India," observed Gaurav. "Take your job as a business."

Sheena smiled in between her puffs, "I know you were always inclined to do your own thing."

"No, not like that. But even when you are employed, you need to think like a businessman. Which sectors are expected to perform well and why? And to move your job towards that way. What do you think, Jai?"

Jai remained silent in the discussion. His participation in the company was always limited to more emotional angles like employee retention or angry customers.

When they returned to the office, Jai realized that the only way to even attempt to reach the target was to make as many cold calls as possible. Even after fifty odd calls, he'd got nothing. The only warm response he got was from Aakash, who asked him to come home on time so that they could catch a movie. But as he was about to leave, the boss came to his desk and dropped a fat file.

"Jai! I need you for an urgent presentation for the North region. You're not leaving?!" snapped boss Amrit, noticing that Jai had cleared his papers and had switched off his computer.

"No sir," Jai grimaced.

"Good…come to my cabin now."

Amrit asked him to prepare a presentation which had nothing to do with his area. But as always, Jai could not find the courage to speak up. He continued working, periodically noticing missed calls from Aakash. The boss finally let him go at 9 p.m. When Jai's phone buzzed again, he noticed that it was from his mother. He thanked God it wasn't the angry Aakash while he answered the phone.

"Hello Maa," Jai said morosely.

"Kya hua beta?" his mother sensed his mood. "Office *mein ho?*"

"Na Maa, bas abhi nikla hun."

"Aaj jaldi nikal gaya beta, office mein kaam kam hai kya?" His mother responded sarcastically and the two of them laughed for the next couple of minutes.

Jai had always been closer to his mother. Her childlike enthusiasm and her maturity to lighten up the situations made him lean towards her in times of stress. But the kinds of stress a person goes through changes with age. To share the stress of passing MBA exams was one thing, but how could he share the stress of achieving targets? Not that his mother ever understood any of his studies during his educational years. For him it was like talking to a mirror, a very supportive and pleasant mirror, and the talking gave him all the energy. But now, he didn't want to upset her so he gave her an optimistic outlook and hung up.

When he got home, Jai got an earful from his roommate. "It's all because of you. People like you who keep their mouths shut get fucked in return!" shouted Aakash after learning about the presentation.

"It's not like that. Things are getting messy. They are planning to fire more people," Jai said softly.

"Aakash! We can go to the movie tomorrow," interrupted Vivek to calm him down.

"I don't care about the movie!" Aakash said as he tore up the movie tickets. "You idiot, how long are you going to suffer like this?"

"I am not doing this on my own. If I don't do it, somebody else will," Jai defended.

"That's the biggest problem. The same companies won't dare ask you to stay back when they operate in the West but when it comes to India, they know that for each seat, they have 2000 applications. God! Why did our forefathers not use condoms?" Aakash further exploded putting the blame on his favourite reason – population.

"I don't think there were enough condoms available back then," smiled Vivek trying to ease things off.

"Yeah. They had some surgery back then. I don't remember what they used to call it."

"Nasbandi!" Jai mentioned hoping to veer the topic away from him.

"Fucker! I still remember the jingle. *'Bas do minute ki pareshaani, zindagi bhar aasani'*. In fact, I recall that I used to sing it while going to play cricket every evening. I remember aunties blushing over it."

"So, you used to bat with Nasbandi on your lips?" retorted Vivek.

"Yeah...I guess so." They cheered up over Vivek's comment.

Aakash back slapped Jai while Vivek watched with compassion. It was times like these that kept them together. Stupid enjoyable moments could only happen with friends.

"I propose we spend the night with the Pandavas," declared Vivek.

"With the Pandavas?" confirmed Aakash surprised as Vivek was the last guy who would propose to do that.

The Mahabharat Lounge

?

Aakash, Jai and Vivek arrived at the lounge an hour before midnight. They paused to re-read the description.

The biggest story ever told in this country's history is the MAHABHARAT. With each distinctive character, it is clear that the epic is a blend of all human traits. From greed to selflessness, doom to glory, hatred to love, jealousy to acceptance, chastity to lust, war to peace, the tale of *Mahabharat* has every shade of emotion woven into it. Therefore, to celebrate this ancient masterpiece, we have opened up *The Mahabharata Lounge* in the heart of our very own Delhi. Please join us and enjoy the glory and spirit of this timeless classic.

There were intricate designs carved on metal fitted on its huge wooden door. It had the panache of the mythological era, a teaser of what to expect indoors. The design was of Arjuna holding a bow and arrow aimed at the bird's eye with a caption: *The Hangover Bird...Fly with it.*

The bouncer let them in. The interior was straight out of the décor from the Mahabharata. Sudarshan Chakras hung from the ceiling, rotating in opposite directions. The walls were draped with images, depicting some of the epic events – the great betting game with cocktails placed next to the gamblers, Lord Krishna giving instructions to a drunken Arjun, Draupadi Chirharan, Bheem drinking from a beer drum, Bheem and Duryodhan's beer drinking contest, Arjun shooting his arrow at a whisky bottle, the war fought at the field of Kurukshetra over eighteen cases of scotch, and many more. The music was fusion, ancient instruments playing modern rhythms. The staff was dressed accordingly. The men in dhotis and pagdis, roamed topless with just gamchas over their muscular shoulders. The women bartenders were sexy in their hip-hugging attires, exposing their curves.

They sat at the bar counter and checked a menu slate. The slate was inscribed on wood. Each cocktail derived its name from a character from Mahabharat.

Blind was an option at the bar. It meant that out of their twelve signature cocktails, you would get the luck of the dice. The waiter dressed like Shakuni Mama showed them the dice.

"Bhaanjon! Should I roll the dice for you?"asked Shakuni Mama. He rolled the dice for each one and handed them their drinks.

Aakash got cocktail no. 4 – The Bhishma Pitahmah Effect. It was a mixture of sour liquors and black rum effectively causing the breath to smell foul, turning girls away, and one would attain temporary chastity. Aakash was not thrilled by the choice. There were many attractive girls on the dance floor. Vivek ended up with Cocktail number 12 – The Bheem factor. With many types of liquor mixed in and very little water, this one was a sure shot quick hit. And Jai got cocktail no 6 – Arjun's dilemma. It represented a cocktail for that part of Arjun's life when he had to live like a woman. Neither here, nor there. And so was the cocktail. A mix of soft and hard liquors. A sip could make you feel lighter and another would give you a sudden kick.

The three friends, consumed by their own suffering, didn't stop with one drink. By the end of the evening they were completely sloshed.

"You are my baby brother; when your boss fucks your ass, it's my ass that bleeds!" cried an emotional Aakash to Jai.

"You are my brother from another mother,"mumbled Jai to complete the gesture of empathy.

"Aakash...I think that girl over there is staring at you,"Vivek pointed at a drunken girl dancing wildly.

Aakash responded even without looking at the girl, "I know...I noticed. She wants my body...but I have played her enough. Girls give music to my life, but tonight is not about me, it's about my brother. Let's fix up a girl for him and take his virginity away," shouted Aakash, slapping Jai's back.

People turned to look and smiled.

"Bro, I am happy with my virginity. It's a gift for my future wife. So shut the fuck up!' Jai hissed, embarrassed.

"Oh my god! Gift! Show me the gift...Have you kept it under wraps?"

"You are completely drunk," declared Vivek.

"No I am not...in fact, I am feeling dry. Let's order something more."

"I think we have had enough."

"Noooo...I want some more." Jai cried out like a small child asking for more milk.

"Okay. But last one...what do you guys want?"

"Since I am feeling horny, I propose that we all go for the Paanchaali!

Paanchali arrived in a big fat pitcher. Five beers offered solace to the moaners.

This was the only bar in town which opened from Suryaast to Suryoday, the only Mahabharat ideology it followed, contradictory to the era it represented. In the wee hours of the morning, the three friends stumbled out. Their movements were awkward and tongues continued to slip with unformed words. But they felt as brave as tigers, not really bothered about being endangered.

Jai felt the urge of making his contribution to the hazy night sky and asked for a smoke from Aakash who joyously complied.

Jai and Aakash lit up. Vivek watched them, feeling left out of this sharing of a smoke. "Won't you ask me to join?" he cried.

"Is it your smoking day today?" Aakash mocked Vivek who fixed specific days for various activities – for eating eggs, chicken, drinking and smoking.

"Yes it is," declared Vivek.

Jai offered him a cigarette while Aakash lit it.

They all smoked in silence and rested on the footpath near a *chouraha*.

Vivek disturbed the peace. "Do you ever think where all the smoke goes?"

"It evaporates," Jai said.

Aakash intervened, "It goes into the air...the atmosphere."

"What if you want it back?" Vivek was in no mood to stop his prodding.

"You can't have it back...it's gone," said Aakash.

Vivek stretched it further, "But why not?"

Aakash tried to make it absolutely clear to him. He gestured as he explained to Vivek. "That's the way it is...you light up...you take a puff... you breathe in...you breathe out...the smoke disappears in the air." They kept looking at the smoke till it disappeared.

"What if you don't breathe out?" continued Vivek.

"That will choke you, my friend. If you want to enjoy the cigarette, you have to let go of the smoke," replied Aakash realizing that Vivek is hinting towards Aarti. No matter how attached Vivek was to Aarti, Aakash knew that the relationship was over, that divorce was imminent and Vivek's delay in accepting his failed relationship was causing the smoke to get stuck.

Jai was particularly impressed with Aakash and decided to do something he was not known for, to break silences and speak his heart out.

"I want to tell you boys something."

"Yeah, go ahead," Aakash and Vivek chorused.

Jai summoned all his courage to speak. He sat on the road across from his friends, stared at them for a while and finally said to Aakash.

"Man...I want to be like you. I like the way you are – full of life, aspirations, enthusiasm. You are your own boss. I want to be like that...I want to flirt around without feeling guilty...I want to speak my mind. I want to live life on my own terms...I want to open up."

Aakash was happy that he could inspire someone and responded, "So then open up...who's stopping you?"

"I don't have a rich father," Jai replied, suddenly swiping away all the praise he had showered.

"Even I don't have a rich father!" Aakash was offended.

"You do have a rich father," Vivek intervened.

"But it's not about money. If you want to open up, just do it."

"That part I agree!" Vivek nodded.

"But how?" Jai asked.

"Tell me something, what if you had money? What would you do?"

Jai was ready with an answer probably practiced several times over. "For starters, I will start my own business, whatever that business might be…but I will be my own boss. Next, I would go to the pub and pick up the first sexy girl who lays eyes on me and spend a passionate night with her."

"And then?" enquired Aakash happy to finally hear such honesty from Jai.

"And then I see myself waking up the next morning feeling guilty," completed Jai. Aakash shook his head in pity while Vivek laughed heartily, not to tease Jai but because he knew Jai better. He was from a similar family background and understood Jai's ethical dilemma.

Vivek kneeled forward and cupped Jai's face in his palms. "My dear friend. You are one of the millions of people who are stuck between Bharat and India. You grew up in Bharat but are now living in India. The moral dilemma is unavoidable."

"But, trust me – Bharat was hypocritical. Go with India," snapped Aakash. Vivek removed the cusp and 'kind of' agreed with Aakash.

Jai pondered for a while, "Hmm…but what about my parents? They still live in Bharat."

"Well, that's a choice you will have to make," shrugged Aakash.

"You were able to make that choice because you had a rich father," Jai brought the discussion back to square one.

The need arose for Akash to defend his independent spirit. "Oh come on! I have not taken a single penny from my dad since I completed my graduation. And even today I survive because of my own savings, not by contributions made by my rich father."

"Don't take it too seriously, Jai,"Vivek said to cool them. "If you want to open up, start with small things."

"Like what?"

"Like start saying no to your boss."

Jai dwelled on his boss's monstrous personality and could not think of doing anything out of character.

"I don't agree. if you want to change your life, you need to take drastic steps," said Aakash.

"Like what?" Jai gazed at his liberated friend.

"Like leave your job and start a business with me."

"Hmm," Jai was lost again in his wandering mind. Vivek intervened.

"Leaving his job would be too drastic for him. I think he should start by confronting his boss. He will develop confidence."

"What purpose will that confidence solve? If he wants to own up his life, he should kick his boss's balls," declared Aakash.

While the two friends continued their debate about whom and where Jai should kick ass, the beer which Jai had consumed by the pitcher was starting to kick into his bladder. But he had bladder shyness, another trait he wanted to overcome. He looked around for a loo, but then thought, *Who am I kidding? This is India.* Then he glanced at the chouraha which was deserted and dark. Another trail of thought, this time a bold one went through his mind: *What better way to open up than by removing my bladder shyness by peeing in the open!* He sauntered towards the chouraha and noticed some stray dogs barking at the sky. But he did not stop, gathered up his courage, reached the chouraha, unzipped his jeans and called out to his friends.

"Listen up well wishers...since you, Vivek, wanted me to take small steps and you, Aakash, wanted me to take drastic steps, I have decided to satisfy you both. For the first time since I gained puberty, I will pee in the open and while I do so, I will make circles and let my fears flow with my soil. Amen."

Aakash and Vivek stopped their discussion and stared at him. Jai rotated his pee and felt liberated as he let go of his fears in the traditional Hindu style.

"OM Amritaya bhasmaaye swaaha…Om jobam bhasmaaye swaaha…. Om garibi bhasmaaye swaaha…. Om Phattu bhasmaaye swaaha…Om virgin bhasmaaye swaaha!"

Aakash watched him with amusement while Vivek expressed his worry. "What is he doing!"

"Getting sexually liberated!" Aakash summed it up accurately.

"Do you think peeing in the open will benefit him?" demanded Vivek.

Jai's test of resilience skidded into his life at an opportune time. The amount of beer he had consumed made sure that his bladder took a while to empty, which not only soaked the chouraha, but also created small rivulets across the adjoining roads.

A young woman riding a scooty happened to pass through the chouraha. She didn't notice the chouraha was drenched. Her scooty skidded and she slipped and fell, injuring her leg.

Jai stopped his unloading midway even though there was some pee still left in his tank. He zipped up. The trio rushed towards her asking her if she was okay. Aakash and Vivek helped her to her feet. She had some bleeding scratches. Jai picked up her scooty and rested it on its stand.

"You want us to take you to a doctor?" Aakash politely asked the damsel in distress.

"No thanks. I am fine. I didn't know it rained today. But strangely, it's wet only around that circle," replied the young woman, a little dazed.

Jai and Aakash exchanged glances. There was a spate of guilty looks between them. Jai particularly was speechless for two reasons – one was the obvious reason that he was guilt ridden, which he always was, but the other was, he found her hot. She was wearing a clingy top and a mini skirt and Jai kept stealing glances at her smooth skin.

"Seriously, we can take you to a hospital or we can also drop you home," Aakash offered not realizing that he did not have his car.

"No thanks. I stay nearby. In fact my friends followed me to the start of this road. Delhi is not a safe place for girls."

She turned down the offer politely but Aakash felt the need to clarify.

"We are not from Delhi," he stated.

Jai took the opportunity to help his victim and kickstarted the scooty to life. She limped up to him and thanked him for his help. Jai felt guilty and yet was mesmerized. She bid them goodbye and disappeared into darkness.

Aakash waited for a while before he could fire Jai. "You ass! You almost killed her."

They all stared at the wet chouraha. Jai's pee had now made it to the far corners of various roads.

Aakash and Vivek expressed their concerns over Jai's pee. "Look at where all your sussu has reached," said Aakash.

Jai looked guilty. "I never imagined something like this could happen."

"But do you feel liberated?" Aakash turned their attention to the purpose of this activity.

"I don't think God wants me to get liberated," Jai concluded glumly.

They walked towards their flat when Jai's foot stepped on something. A sound similar to cracking glass resonated. Jai leaned down and realized that his shoe had landed on a mobile phone and broken it.

"Oh no! It must be that scooty girl's. The entire screen is smashed," Jai checked the broken mobile phone.

"Great! First you broke her, and now her phone," Aakash commented.

"What should I do?" Jai wondered aloud.

"Keep it with you for now, and return it to her tomorrow," said Vivek.

"But to whom will I return it? We didn't even ask her name."

Vivek patted him, "Search for names like Home, Mummy, Papa in the phone book."

Jai nodded. "Oh yeah! Good idea! She must definitely have parents…I mean how else can someone make it to this world?"

Okay

The alarm rang for the sixth time, but Aakash showed no signs of life. Vivek was trying to meditate, and found the intermittent sounds irritating. Vivek entered his room, shook him violently by his shoulders and shouted.

"Wake up!"

Aakash slowly opened his sleepy eyes, which were practically glued together. "What's the time?" he asked, his eyes so red it would bring shame to an angry Rajinikanth.

" It's two in the afternoon!"

"Why did you wake me up so early?"

"It's not early, idiot! Your alarm has been trying to wake you up for the past half an hour."

"So what? Why did you ruin my sleep?

"Ruin your sleep? You ruined my yoga. The moment I tried to concentrate, your mobile played a cheap double meaning song."

"Come on! I slept at five this morning."

"We all slept at the same time and now it's afternoon which means you've had ample sleep."

"Okay okay! I am getting up. Don't do the sleep math." Aakash got up with his eyes closed and rested his shoulder against the headboard.

"By the way, what's the point of the alarm?"

"I need to meet an investor. Do you want to know the business idea?"

"Since you insist, what is it about?" Vivek was curious. He was intrigued by Aakash's wild ideas. The guy had passion and didn't seem deterred by any setbacks. With all the failures Aakash had faced, anyone else would have fallen into self-pity mode. Vivek was, in a way, inspired by Aakash's optimism. If only Vivek could find something to fulfil his own potential.

"Flavoured condoms. Huge and growing market in India, and with people exploring different tastes and different cuisines, the demand is going to grow further."

"Interesting." Vivek frowned, and bit his tongue.

"The uniqueness is in my distribution plan," continued Aakash with eyes closed.

"Go ahead. I am listening."

"I plan to come up with condom vending machines and install them in schools, colleges and call centres."

"What? Isn't that insane?"

"Why? That's where most of the action happens and most of it unprotected?"

"Colleges and call centres. I can still understand, even though I don't think anybody would allow you to do so. But schools...I mean who starts off in a school?"

"I did!"

"Oh yes...I forgot that you went to school as well," taunted Vivek. Aakash opened his left eye to react to his taunt. "Where is my coffee?"

Vivek tried to respond but realized that it was better to make some coffee than listen to his unconvincing idea. He tried to move out but was thrown another question by his sleepy friend. "And where is our boy with his special gift?"

"He has gone to return the broken mobile to the broken girl," Vivek said.

"Good for him! And by the way, those songs are not double meaning songs. They have a deep rooted philosophy in them."

"Now I understand why you want to get into flavoured condoms."

•

Jai met the young woman at a coffee shop. In his excitement, he arrived early, properly attired and clean-shaved – something which he no longer wanted to do on weekdays. He sat nervously. It was not the first time that he was meeting a strange girl. But something was different about today's meeting. He tossed his thoughts around to find out the reason for his discomfort, when suddenly he looked up and saw her make an entry. She was wearing a red kurta with churidaar and he realized his heart flutter as their eyes met.

"Hi!" she called out recognizing him instantly.

"Hi!" replied Jai realizing that his 'hi' was more Hindi than English. She joined him.

"How are you?" asked Jai. He raised his right hand forward for a handshake but hesitated in between.

"I am good. I was confused which one of the three guys would be coming," she said.

"I am Jai!" he managed to say.

"Hi! I am Sneha!"

"How is your leg now?"

"It's fine, just some bruises. Thanks for the help."

"That's fine. Anybody else would have done so."

"I don't know. My dad was very angry. I guess it was too late for a girl to be out alone."

"I guess so."

There was an awkard pause. Then the silence crept in and he found himself staring continuously at the menu card.

"You want to have some coffee?"

"No thanks," she replied. "I will just make a move. Can I have my phone please?"

"Yeah sure! Here it is." Jai took out her phone which now lacked the identity of being called one.

"Oh! It's completely smashed."

"Yes, quite a fall it had."

"I hate the rains!" she said in irritation.

"Why blame the rains? People throw water out of their houses all the time."

"But which jerk would throw water at 4 a.m.?"

Jai decided to remain silent and not mention his effort at sexual liberation.

"Anyway, I should get going," declared Sneha.

"Okay," replied Jai, regretting it immediately.

He thought of an excuse of getting her back into a conversation and just about managed to come up with one before she rose from her seat. "So, you were returning from a pub?"

"Yeah...the Lounge."

"The Mahabharat Lounge?"

"Yeah."

"That's amazing...we were also returning from the same place."

"Oh really? How come we didn't meet there? I guess it is a big place."

"But it's a small world."

"Yeah, guess so!" Sneha nodded with a smile with just the slightest tinge of a blush. Wow! Her first blush! The Mahabharat Lounge seemed to be working. He would stay on the topic.

"So what do you like most about that lounge?"

"The cocktails."

"Which one is your favourite?"

"I like Kurukshetra."

"Oh...that's quite something. Eighteen liquors in one glass."

"I just take one of that and I am through. Which one do you prefer?"

"I like Arjun. Have you tried the Krishna Leela?"

"It's only for couples I think. No, not tried it yet."

Jai was proud of himself for discovering that she didn't have a boyfriend.

"I should really get going now."

"Okay," said Jai, again regretting to miss an opportunity to chat further. Why the hell did he need to say okay to everything? This was not his office. He had to stop her.

"So what do you do?" Jai blurted.

"I am a school teacher."

"That's really nice. A noble profession." He recalled that his parents were looking desperately for a school teacher wife to bring some balance to their son's otherwise imbalanced life.

"Thanks! what about you?"

"I work in a telecom company in the sales department."

"That's cool," replied Sneha.

"Where do you teach?"

"I teach in Ultra Modern School just down the road."

"And you stay nearby?"

"Yeah."

Nope! She was not going to give him her address. End of conversation. Jai noticed his hand on the menu card.

"Have you tried their pasta?" Jai enquired noticing a new item.

"No. Is it good?"

"We can find out if you want to share some."

Sneha smiled and blushed. Another victory! And then their eyes met. The moment which went on for a few seconds was new for Jai – a new feeling, renewed hope, energy to continue running for targets. They spent some time together with a plate of pasta, two cups of coffee and stealing meaningful glances. Jai realized that something inevitable was about to happen.

Desire Leads to Satire

Still suffering from the night's fun, Aakash soothed his red eyes with the help of a few eye drops. Dressed in a suit with neatly gelled hair, he looked mature for his age. His height and his toned physique were impressive when he dressed formally. He waited in the coffee shop of the five-star-hotel where the investor, Mr Sanjay Mehta had arranged the meet. It was already a few minutes past the appointed time. Aakash had heard from his sources that Sanjay was a shrewd businessman. He waited patiently, rehearsing the opening line of his business idea. He was finally led to Sanjay Mehta's table. Aakash greeted him and took a seat, rehearsing the line one last time.

"How are you?" Sanjay asked, more out of politeness.

"I am good, thank you."

"How is you father?"

"He is fine," responded Aakash. His Dad's reference gave a different flavour to the otherwise straight meeting.

"Coffee?"

"Sure. Thanks."

Sanjay ordered a coffee for Aakash. "So, Aakash...what's up these days?"

"Well, finding support to get my start-up funded."

"Sure...what is the idea?"

"The idea is to open up comic book coffee shops throughout India. The Indian comic book market is expanding every year. The success of comic conventions is evidence of this fact. If you enter any bookstore, you find a big comic section now. Superman, Spiderman, Batman – you name it and the comic books have penetrated across the country. What we lack are comic book coffee shops where people can have a coffee and read comics for free. Better than coffee shops currently present where people can only chat."

Sanjay came up with the word which described his disinterest in a subtle manner. "Interesting! Do you have a detailed plan?"

"I can take you through it…" Aakash began by opening his bag.

"You can email it to me…I will go through it in detail," Sanjay cut him short and came back to his hidden agenda of the meeting.

"So, how is Srivastava Saheb?"

"He is doing fine," replied Aakash realizing that this entire meeting was a sham.

"Still in Lucknow? I heard he is handling the UP Health Department now."

"I have no idea."

"Come on Aakash! You should take interest in your Dad's job. It can serve all your purposes."

Aakash understood his implication.

Sanjay finally came clean.

"Here is the deal. We want to expand our medical business. The UP govt is planning to introduce mobile medical vans to cater to all the villages and small towns, and they are looking for a private party association. It's a big deal – a hundred or a hundred and fifty crores. Talk to your dad about this deal and if this gets through, I will fund your coffee shops."

"Sir, the idea I am talking about is a three hundred crore valuation idea. We don't need to run after sarkari jokers to earn money," Aakash replied, aware of Sanjay's response but irritated by the fact that his dad's influence haunted him everywhere.

Sanjay laughed. "You must have heard about that phrase: 'A bird in hand is worth two in the bush'. I am sure you've done your research, but let us try and be a bit more realistic."

"I heard you last month at the Angel Network where you spoke on taking risks and you mentioned this quote. 'A ship in harbour is safe, but that is not what ships are for.'"

Sanjay laughed again over Aakash's naivety. "I agree, Aakash, but that is just for motivating youngsters. You and I are two mature men. We understand that when it comes to money, you need to be cautious."

Aakash nodded in frustration. "You are right. Moneyed men are always right," he clipped. He left in silent rage. As soon as he exited the hotel, his cell phone rang. It was his father.

Speak of the devil. Ever since Aakash was a child, he and his father never had a common agenda. Even in his growing years, when India got globalized and his IAS father was shifting ministries to reap the fruits of development, they had always argued. For his father, development was driven by bureaucrats, while he always believed that entrepreneurs were driving the country ahead.

This often led to a clash between them as his father had always pushed him to get through the IAS, but his mother would intervene and pacify them. Until an unfortunate day when he lost her to typhoid. From that time, the buffer between father and son disappeared, and they could not live together under the same roof. As soon as Aakash finished college, he moved out and focused on proving that he was not his father's son.

The phone stopped ringing and Aakash wondered how he was able to come up with a spate of bitter memories in an instant. The phone rang again. He answered.

"Good evening Dad," Aakash said.

"Hi Aakash, good evening. Where have you been?"

Veiled taunts. "I have been busy."

"I am sure! So, what's new? Any new development?"

"Not really. How is your health?" Aakash asked more like an obligation as his dad was nearing his retirement.

"I am the Secretary of the Health Ministry so my health has got to be fine," his father laughed alone and then continued.

"Listen, I have a fantastic offer for you. I have a friend here, Mr Mahajan, a big industrialist. His reach is spread out in telecom, real estate, and health. He has a lovely daughter. Why don't both of you meet up? You will like her. She is your type – talks about being a self-made person."

Aakash understood what his dad meant. A man who had always taken his service as a business opportunity could only think about settling the failure of his son by getting him married to a big business family.

"Yeah, I get you perfectly, Dad."

"Trust me son. This will be the best decision of your life. When I was struggling with finances years ago, your grandfather got me posted to the Housing Board in Delhi, that's how networking works. I have only two years of service left, let's be smart enough to use it. Come to Lucknow, spend some time with your old dad as well. It's been a while that we met."

"Two years," Aakash said softly, as he was taken back to memories of his father's boastful tales of how he had lured the daughter of a High Court Judge.

"I am driving right now Dad...I will speak to you later."

•

Vivek stood in front of Aarti's house, hesitating to press the door bell. But, this nervosity was very different from the anticipation he had felt when he had met her for the first time. He finally rung the doorbell and she opened it almost immediately. A fair, medium built Brahmin girl who always wore a sari, Aarti was the ideal housewife who was probably hoping for her husband to ask her to return. They sat in the comfortable jute chairs in the verandah while she served him adrak chai and samosas – his favourites. He was slightly elated by these signs. She was attired in his favourite yellow sari too.

"How have you been?" Vivek asked.

"I am fine. You wanted to talk?" Aarti asked straight away.

"I have got a small gift...Happy Anniversary!" Vivek held out a small nicely packed gift.

"I can't take this," she replied quickly.

"Why not?"

"What's the point? We clearly decided to get separated."

"I got the divorce papers you had sent," Vivek's eagerness fizzled as he heard the word *separated*. Aarti maintained a stony silence while Vivek continued.

"Don't you want to give it another chance?" He asked his heart pounding heavily.

"It won't solve any purpose; do you really know what you want from this marriage? Do you even know what you want from life?"

"Nobody knows what they want from their lives. We all live in a reactive society."

"Even then, people live their lives. They don't run around astrologers and religious gurus to understand themselves."

"So, it's all about my job and money?"

"It's much more than that, Vivek. It's about your vulnerability…your madness."

Vivek lost his cool at madness. "That's not madness Aarti, that's exploration!"

Aarti had a tough expression. Vivek calmed himself down, mentally reciting a shloka. "Look, I am sorry. Ultimately it's your life, but what I was trying to do was to find the true purpose of living."

"But I don't want to find out 'Why am I here?'. I know I am already here and I want to live my life to the fullest."

She leaned forward. "Vivek, why can't we just move on? I am sure your gurus have taught you to let go."

Vivek was at a loss for words. It was over. Aarti was not going to heed anymore. It was pointless to even try to propagate a lost cause. He left in silence. Heading towards the main road, he suddenly changed his mind about getting an auto and decided to walk towards his house. It was going to be a long walk, but he needed the time to ponder over his marriage – the one failure in his life. His acaedemic and professional life had inspired and instilled all qualities in him to succeed in every endeavor he undertook, but the one aspect he had not been taught was to surrender.

•

Jai slogged the entire day at various client offices and reached his workplace in the evening. It had been a bad day. He had received negative responses from most of the prospective clients. He slipped into his work station. However, as soon as he opened the glass door, Gaurav greeted him with a message that the boss had been looking for him. Jai headed to Amrit's cabin and noticed that there were four other senior staff members present. They all looked in the middle of an intense animated discussion. Amrit noticed him and gestured that he should enter. A conversation was in progress. Jai listened quietly fuming at this inanity.

Guy 1 started, "I am telling you there is nothing better than the third thela – the kind of elaichi tea he makes is phenomenal."

Guy 2 took it forward. "Hey...did you try the bhelpuri stall?"

Guy 1 was drooling with excitement. "Where exactly?"

Guy 2 smiled. "It's right behind the chole-kulche waala stall."

Guy 1 was all starry-eyed. "How is it?"

Guy 2 smiled."It's awesome. We tried it the other day. Amrit and I went down to discuss the new distribution strategy for prepaid."

"I bet the bhelpuri waala also grabbed the strategy!" Amrit added his two-bits causing a round of laughter. Jai did not get the joke but framed up a fake smile on is face. 'Senior Fucking Management' Jai summarized the jokers in Aakash's language.

The strategic discussion on tea and snacks carried on for a few more minutes. When they finally left, Amrit indicated to Jai to be seated.

"What kind of an ass do you have?" started Amrit. Jai remained silent.

Amrit continued. *"Aaj sabki phaadi hai...socha teri bhi thodi udhed dun."*

"Any problem, sir?" Jai showed fake concern.

Amrit stated. *"Upar se bahut pressure hai.* More pink slips to come. This meeting happened for that purpose. Everybody is so tense. *Tum londe lafadon ko to phir bhi naukri mil jayegi.* Think of a senior guy with family, kids and loans."

"Sir, are they letting people at senior levels also go?"

"At all levels, boss! Nobody to be spared...not even me."

Jai felt a strange sense of relief hearing Amrit's ass was also on the line.

"Tell me Jai? Why should I not fire you?"

A startled Jai came up with the most expected answer. "You know my track, sir."

"I know that and that's the reason you have been given this wonderful opportunity to speak."

"Sir, I have met and crossed all my targets."

"The targets are going to increase ten folds now. Do you think you can handle that?"

"Sir?" a confused Jai asked.

"I told you these are tough times, slog your ass out, and stay all night in office if required. I have spared you with a lower target. Everybody was saying four, but I have managed you a three." With that, he gestured to Jai to leave.

Jai left and bumped into an equally disgruntled Sheena. The only guy who seemed relaxed was Gaurav.

"They are going to fire around five hundred more," blurted Gaurav.

"Oh God! Why don't they just shut down?" moaned Sheena.

"They are planning to sell off, reduce costs, show profits so that they get a good price," Gaurav explained.

"And we all will be sold out with the company?" asked Jai.

"You would be lucky if you get sold out with the company," Gaurav replied with a smile.

"And how many senior guys will be thrown out?" Sheena enquired.

"A couple."

Jai found this outrageous. Amrit had made it seem like everybody was under equal pressure. Like any war, the soldiers operating at the lowest lines would be killed even though the goof ups were at the level of the highest offices.

Sheena invited Jai and Gaurav to her place for drinks so that they could crib further, but Jai wanted to avoid the cribbing session, and he had other plans with Sneha.

Butter Chicken – My Staple Diet

The coffee plan between Jai and Sneha went well and soon graduated to a dinner date at a dhaba recommended by him.

Jai arrived at the dhaba slightly late and found her waiting. As soon as she noticed him, she gave him a warm smile. The whiteness of her small teeth, the redness of her medium thick lips, warmth of her black eyes decorated with kajal and the serenity of her face made him forget all his troubles.

"Are you sure you want to eat here?" a concerned Sneha pointed out.

"Yeah...the food is amazing."

"Doesn't seem to be the kind of place you should be taking a new friend."

Jai noticed her concern but didn't need to defend the place when a Mercedes arrived and two couples got off the car.

"Hey, don't feel insecure...the gentry is really good here," Jai reassured her.

Sneha smiled and they entered. Jai ordered and was doubly pleased with the fact that she was a chicken lover. He placed the order of his staple – dal makhani, butter chicken and tandoori rotis.

"You are a Punju right?" Sneha commented.

"Yeah...how did you guess?"

"By the food you ordered."

"Oh...I thought you guessed it from my vibrant good looks."

"Someone is in love with himself!"

"I mean that's what people say about me."

"So you are fair...that's one attribute. Medium built, that's another attribute of being a Punju. But what about the height?"

"What about it? I am five feet, eight-and-a-half inches."

"You're short."

"Hey, come on, all Punjabis are not tall. Stop teasing me," Jai laughed.

The food arrived and they gorged on the delicacies. Jai's cellphone vibrated repeatedly. These were calls from his office. Jai didn't want to spoil the perfect moment so he let it ring.

"So how is work?" Sneha asked.

"It's fine." Jai tried to be casual about it.

"You know I started my career in a bank."

"Oh really?"

"I worked there for an year, then got bored. I wanted to live a more meaningful and relaxed life than running around for targets and customers. Now, I teach young kids, and I get free by afternoon and then I paint. I enjoy my life." She shrugged.

"Good for you. But everyone is not so lucky; there are people like me who need to earn for their family."

"I understand Jai, but then it's all about choices. Most of my friends still work in corporates and have fancy cars while I have a scooty. They visit places like the Lounge every week while I go once in a month. But they are more stressed out, and whenever we meet, they keep cribbing about their work while I am cool and relaxed."

"So what do you think I should do?"

"Just follow your heart."

"It's not as easy as it sounds," replied Jai and then smiled. "Or maybe it is easy, like how I followed my heart and asked you out."

Sneha blushed and gave him a smile that melted his heart.

Player or Playee?

?

Jai reached home late after dinner, aiming to complete a sales report. Leaving office early was going to cost him the night.

As he reached home, he found Aakash and Vivek in the middle of a heated conversation.

"But, what did the investor finally tell you?" Vivek asked Aakash.

"He asked me to forward the PowerPoint presentation and that he will think about it."

"Do that! What's the big deal?"

"Have you not been listening? I told you he is more interested in that government deal. He is not even going to open the presentation." Aakash said in irritation.

"What do you want from me?"

"Open up your network for me – your IIM network, your investor network."

"I am not in touch with any of them. These networks are live till the time you are in action."

"Then get back into action!" Aakash reasoned with Vivek, showing concern. Aakash had pushed him to start a business together. Vivek was good at strategizing and networking. And he realized that if he did not divert his focus elsewhere, then he was certainly heading towards depression.

Vivek was silent. He understood Aakash's concerns. But the failure of his marriage had drained him of any energy to get involved in any work.

Silence engulfed the two, while Jai stood by awkwardly. "Which new business are you planning to get into?"

"Flavored condoms manufacturing plant," stated Aakash.

"I don't think you will be able to earn profits."

"Why?"

Aakash was already irritated.

"Because you will end up using most of them. I have seen your phone directory. It's filled up with Ps and Ns." Jai guffawed while Vivek's face finally cracked a smile.

"What are Ps and Ns?" Vivek asked.

"Pooja and Neha, the most commonly used girl names"

"Don't you dare peep into my phone directory again," retorted Aakash.

"Why not? You ate most of the pinnis my mother had sent for me."

"How can you equate pinnis with phone book?"

"And how can you think of manufacturing condoms?"

Aakash snapped out the truth. "Guys, I was just joking, I am not planning to manufacture condoms, I plan to open up comic book coffee shops instead."

Jai continued with his excitement of changing the mood and commented, "Oh...I love comics."

"So, what's the investment size?" demanded Vivek ignoring Jai's childish remark.

But Jai continued, "My favorite is Dhruv. But I also like Chacha Chaudhary, Billu and Pinki."

Aakash decided to ignore him as well. "It's five plus."

"That's quite a lot," declared Vivek.

"Jab Sabu ko gussa aata hai to kahin jwaala mukhi footta hai." Jai was in his own world.

"Have you gone mad?" Aakash found it difficult to ignore him anymore.

"That's how I react when my ass is on fire," claimed Jai.

"Why?"

"My target just got revised from 1.5 to 3 crores."

"That's insane, it's like someone masturbating on the tallest building of the world and expecting his semen to land on the moon." Aakash summed it.

"That was quite thoughtful," appreciated Jai and continued. "Thinking about what you just said…do you think the semen will reach the ground or evaporate while falling?"

"That's an interesting question…let's ask Vivek…he is an engineer." Both look at Vivek for an answer.

"I think not only will the semen hit the ground, but it will also travel through drains to the dark corners of the underground where it will meet cheapsters like the both of you." Vivek ranted on knowing that his friends will never change. "But, going back to your concern, that's the trick with these companies. They create a lot of stress around jobs so that you don't crib about increments and bonuses later on."

"Oh! So you think they are doing it so that we don't expect any increments and are just happy that we still have jobs."

"Exactly!"

"I think I should express myself on Facebook. Sheena has done that on FB and Twitter," Jai said.

"Any joker can express himself on FB. Go face your ass of a boss and express it," Aakash said.

Jai was silent.

"It's okay. Just go and change," Vivek said.

"But that's so cheap. They are playing around with our lives."

"That's the difference between an employer and an employee. One is a player and the other a playee," Aakash jumped in again to make his point.

"What's a playee?"

"You will know what I mean."

Balls of Laddoos

Dark clouds surrounded the outdoors, and indoors. The atmosphere was tense as pink slips were distributed. Such a ruthless use of the colour of love can only be seen in a corporate office. Some good, some bad, some wanted, some unwanted staff were royally thrown out of the company. Amrit was firing some senior employees. He had never been so polite in his conversations. But even his politeness had a feeling of coldness about it.

Three conference rooms were dedicated to slaughter employees. Jai and Sheena sat next to each other at their work stations. They tried to focus on work. They saw Gaurav being really pally with Amrit and he had a list of employees to be fired. Jai was both jealous and pitiful at the same time.

"I think Gaurav is responsible for Pradeep getting fired," Sheena whispered.

"Don't think like that," Jai tried to calm her.

"Seriously, he is holding the list. I am sure he would have suggested names."

"Yeah, he would have given suggestions, but not of Pradeep."

"Jai, he does not like him."

"I know they have some differences, but he won't get him fired. Besides, there are so many other people losing their jobs. Look at Akshat, he was hired just six months ago. What was the point of hiring him in the first place?"

"Poor chap! He won't get a job anywhere else easily. We all are paying for the CEO's greed. Son of a bitch wanted fast growth, fast expansion, and hire and fire in six months. I am sure he would not have given nine months to his wife to deliver his baby."

"Do you think you will be able to achieve the targets?" Jai asked, trying to change the topic.

"I won't even try to achieve it. If they want to fire me, so be it."

"Gutsy you! You have a husband to take care of your expenses," Jai brought back the discussion to money.

"You don't a need husband for that, you need balls!" An answer similar to that of Sneha's, but a bit more impolite.

Amrit suddenly emerged from his cabin and called out to Jai. Jai glanced at Sheena. Everything suddenly seemed to be going in slow motion. As Jai got out of his seat, he thought of his parents, his average academics, and the fees that his parents paid. His feet slowed when he thought of the moral responsibilities towards his parents. He walked at a snail's pace when he realized that he would be at a loss if he lost this job. He reluctantly made his way to Amrit's cabin.

"Phati kyun padi hai?" Amrit queried.

"Nothing like that, sir," Jai responded feebly.

"I want you to consolidate the sales reports for entire North India."

"Sure sir," Jai responded with unusual enthusiasm. Never before had he loved consolidating the reports so much. He exited and gave Sheena a thumbs up signal. He quickly got down to consolidating the report, calling up the sales heads of various states and filling up the excel sheet. Jai was thinking about his parents again, glad that he would be sending them the chunk of his salary. He completely blanked out from his surroundings in relief. So much so that he didn't hear Sheena's name being called. Only when she was at his desk did he realize with a sense of horror what had happened. Sheena faced him with tears in her eyes. He had been self-absorbed and felt awful.

He got out of his seat to console her as she tried to control her tears. She started to pack her stuff – her birthday cards pinned to the wall, her family picture, her Ganesha idol, and her awards and certificates. Tears kept rolling down her cheeks as she emptied her desk. She took her lunch bag out and gave Jai a small box. "I brought these laddoos for you."

Jai didn't know how to react, but he took the box. She proudly walked out of the office. Jai noticed Gaurav and Amrit watching her leave. It hit him a little later that he should have at least seen her off till the parking lot. He quickly ran outside. She was still there, trying to open her car and talking on her phone, probably with her husband. "I know sweetie…it's good for our kids."

"What did he say?" asked Jai.

"Not he, they said. I told you Gaurav is playing games. He is going to be your next boss."

"What? His numbers were lower than mine."

"Not anymore."

"Do you think he recommended your name?"

"I don't know that. I just realized that despite all the hardwork, college was much easier than this corporate world."

He looked at Sheena as she sat in her car and gave life to the engine. She rolled down her window to complete what she meant. "It was performance minus politics in college. Here it's just the opposite."

She drove out of the parking as Jai continued to gape.

Chaddi Buddy

It continued to rain heavily as Jai struggled through roads clogged with cars and water. This was the first time that he was not in a mood to enjoy the rains. His friends waited for him, playing cards and enjoying pakodas with rum. He arrived home in a glum mood.

"Hey lover boy, got all wet and dirty?" Aakash asked, glad to see Jai.

"Only wet I guess." Vivek snickered.

Jai gave them a bleak smile.

"Come on join us! Get a glass," called out Aakash.

"No, thanks. I am tired and want to sleep," replied Jai and moved to his room.

"He sounds depressed," said Aakash.

"Yeah...probably some problem in office."

"I hope they didn't revise his target further."

"I will go and talk to him."

"I'll come along."

"No! You stay here," Vivek instructed and headed towards Jai's room.

He caught Jai in the midst of changing clothes. Jai unloaded his mental burden along with his clothes.

"What do you think is the worst thing? (shoes dumped). The office was converted into a slaughter house today (socks removed). The employees were called and ripped off their jobs (shirt thrown). You know the whole atmosphere was so suffocating (belt unleashed). I felt like running away (vest flung). And the worst part was that there was no logic (trousers dropped), even performers like Sheena got knocked. (Jai reached for his underwear but stopped). I saw the company in its entire nakedness," completed Jai, finally taking a breath, standing almost naked before Vivek.

Aakash had followed Vivek and stood outside the room listening to Jai. He could not help but interfere.

"So, what now?" Aakash asked as he entered the room.

"I have lost my ability to think," declared Jai.

"Just relax, the damage is already done. Just try and accept it," said Vivek to pacify him.

"Accept what? I think he should go and kick the ass of that boss of his," snapped Aakash.

"What difference would that make? This is the harsh economic reality of today's world," stated Vivek.

"Then change the economic reality and build your own economy," shouted Aakash giving the discussion his favourite turn.

"Listen guys, I just want to sleep."

"Atleast eat some pakodas," suggested Vivek.

"I don't feel like eating anything."

"My friend, I am with you in your sorrow," Aakash comforted Jai.

"I know. Thanks."

"No, my friend, you didn't get me. I am really with you in your sorrow," Aakash continued and started shedding his clothes to join him.

"What are you doing?" Vivek shrieked.

"I suggest you too take your clothes off and let's have a warm dinner in our undies, that will strengthen our relationship," said Aakash with excitement.

"Are you insane?"

"When I was in college, we had this custom of having our dinner in our undies if any of our hostel buddies got laid. Oh boy! I remember the entire month of February, we just could not have dinner in our night suits. We really became close as a group, we stood there for each other, be it in the cold or mosquitoes or the humiliation we faced because of the holes in our undies.

"That's a very touching story, you never shared it with us," commented Jai, feeling emotional.

But Vivek was adamant. "No! Not me, you guys can go have your dinner in your undies, I am fine."

"Come on Vivek, don't be a spoilsport," asked Jai.

"How will eating in my undies help?"

Both Aakash and Jai stood in front of Vivek making him feel overdressed. Peer pressure.

•

The three men dressed in nothing but their undies and took their seats around a centre table in the drawing room. Aakash was completely at ease in his underwear, remembering the good old days, while Jai initially hesitant, started relaxing. Vivek was clearly uncomfortable.

"This mirchi pakoda is really good. It has mirchi in it but is still not spicy, want to know why?" Aakash said. Jai and Vivek didn't bother responding, but he still continued. "That's because the mirchi has been fried; when you fry it, all the unnecessary spice goes away leaving just the taste you relish. That's true with the pains of life as well."

As soon as he mentioned the word "pain", both Jai and Vivek looked up as he explained further. "If you fry your pains, eat those fried pains, you start enjoying. Even more so, mix them up with some witty chutney."

"Can you stop your philosophical crap?" retorted Vivek.

"It's not crap! It's reality. Let me tell you another reality. Do you know where these pakodas have come from?"

"From the market?" replied Jai.

"Yes, but from which market?"

"I don't know."

"Come on, guess?"

"Okay, I lose."

"Let me explain – we got these pakodas from the sector market where we stay."

"Great!" said Jai.

"Yes, great. That market which only a couple of months back used to be a barren place with some vacant shops has now blossomed into a lively market, and you know why? I will tell you why. Because some saint opened up an angrezi-sharaab-ki-dukaan. In just two months, you have a pakoda stall, a non-veg stall, a ration shop and not to forget an ATM – that's what I call economic growth."

Even though Jai and Vivek were silent, they did ponder over what he just said.

"And to appreciate my point even better, I have a surprise for you guys this coming Saturday," announced Aakash.

"What is it about?" Vivek asked.

"It's about us."

King Proudy

The stage set-up was elaborate and the entire hall was full of energy. This was the place of inspiring stories. Successful entrepreneurs from across the country gathered and addressed aspiring entrepreneurs. This was also a place where good ideas were married to money. If any budding entrepreneur had an interesting idea, they could try convincing the angel investors.

Aakash had brought Jai and Vivek for a dual purpose – to motivate Jai and to convince Vivek. While Jai, a first-timer, liked the feel of the place, Vivek on the other hand was not a newcomer to such forums and was impatient and irritated.

"Why have you got us to this show-off platform?" demanded Vivek.

"I know there is nothing new for you here, but look at our little Jai – he looks so excited."

Jai had gone ahead and checked the brochure filled with the schedule of various speakers. The brochure had businessmen and women from all walks of life. A twenty-eight-year-old computer whiz kid who created a profitable business out of hacking, an owner of a restaurant chain, a husband and wife running a business teaching students in America from India, and many more. It seemed like a world of endless opportunities. Jai suddenly felt his job stress and office politics was petty.

Vivek noticed his excitement and decided to play along. Jai looked like a child who had come to the zoo for the first time.

The session started with a father-son duo. The father had started his journey as a barber giving people hair-cuts by a riverside in a village. He eventually moved to Delhi and rented a small shop, occasionally helped by his only son. As his son finished his education, he introduced new services in the shop. Business grew and they moved to a posh locality. They introduced franchises. Today, the duo had a chain of hair styling saloons across the country with an annual turnover of two hundred crores.

"Please welcome the man who changed the way Indians cut their hair...Mr Palash Jain!" the host announced. Palash Jain, a youthful guy spoke with sophisticated enthusiasm.

"Hi everyone! My name is Palash Jain, PJ. And it was actually a PJ to think of opening up a chain of barber shops, especially when you've completed your MBA from IIM and started your career as an investment banker."

Aakash glanced at Vivek to see whether he had noticed the similarity, but Vivek shrugged. "So, five years ago, when I decided to chuck my corporate career and expand my Dad's business, I was referred to as '*Nai*' by my colleagues. But I didn't mind because your intelligence, wherever it is, comes underneath that mop of hair on your head. Contrary to the general belief that business is all about balance sheets and numbers crunching, I believe business is more about relationships – relationships with your employees, your customers and your society. And when these relationships become stronger, balance sheets become legal formalities. For it is the joy of living in those relationships that takes these businesses forward. In any business, the ultimate measure of success is not the bottomline, but happy customers. And as far as money is concerned, when you boast of a two hundred crore turnover, the same investment bankers want to give you a head massage. My only advice to the youth of this country is to follow their hearts, for the heart finds a way which is much more logical than all the brains of the world put together. Looking back, I can only proudly say that, 'My father is a Nai, and so am I'."

The entire hall erupted with applause and gave him a standing ovation. Jai was extremely excited and thanked Aakash for bringing them here. More sessions followed. One of the speakers spoke on the importance of contagious enthusiasm.

"Enthusiasm is contagious. It is like a virus. Go get infected with it and spread the infection wherever you can. Let it spread in your veins and your body. And you know the best part of enthusiasm? Unlike AIDS, *ye chhune se failta hai*."

Another standing ovation for the speaker who taught entrepreneurship at various management institutes. Vivek was particularly excited listening to the professor as it reminded him of spirituality and the world being one.

It was at lunch time that the three of them discussed the speeches. For the first time they were least interested in the delicacies on the table. They shook hands with some of the speakers and were lucky enough to get a couple of contact numbers.

Some more sessions continued in the second half with a special guest coming in around 5 p.m. The guest was a first generation entrepreneur who had attained cult status not just because of his business skills, but also because of his flamboyant lifestyle, not to forget the fleet of girls which hovered around him. He walked in with four stunning women, two on each arm, acting as his bodyguards. He held a cigar in his right hand and a glass of champagne in his left hand. He climbed the stairs of the stage and was given a standing ovation. Since both his hands were occupied, one of the girls accompanying him held the mike.

The host welcomed him, but his voice was muffled under the roar of support from the audience.

"Ladies and gentlemen, please welcome the dynamic, the charming, one and only, owner of The Bang group – Mr Proudyuman Lahiri, popularly known as Proudy."

Proudy stated, "I am not here to give you any gyaan. I am sure you've had an overdose since morning. I am here to invite you for a party. I am throwing a big party tonight and all of you are invited."

The whole crowd went mad with excitement and continued with their clapping and cheering.

"Let's meet tonight and change the definition of sexy. People keep asking me what's sexier: these beautiful girls or the bottomline of my businesses. But I tell them the sexiest is when I explore new businesses. It's when youngsters like you take their ideas to new heights. Sexy is nothing but a state of mind and my state of mind is always sexy."

Proudy gestured a thumbs up to everybody as he exited the stage, only to be followed by a throng of fans.

•

The whole excitement of entrepreneurship shifted to the excitement of attending Proudy's party. His parties were famous for being lavish, extravagant and full of desirable women. That night the ambience of the party was amazing. The three friends had never seen so many beautiful girls under one roof. The décor was classy, the food had as much range as flora and fauna and the booze – well it flowed like water from the Jal Board tanker. They introduced themselves to other guys who had attended the conference. Jai found a lot of people from the corporate sector just waiting for that big idea to take the plunge.

"This is what I call life! Fucking awesome life! You do business with the best people, earn big money, party, and then get laid with the prettiest women," Aakash said with excitement.

"Did you look at the confidence of Rajesh Sharma? He's just twenty-five and he has already sold his company for ten million dollars!" Jai was stuck with this success story when Rajesh was called on stage. Jai's dream had been to make it big at an early age, ensuring his parents retired comfortably.

"This is just the beginning, bro. There is an entire universe of people making it big, you just need to get into the network."

"I think I am ready to get into this network."

"And tonight you will be amazed to find out how many people make it really big just because of their networks. Vivek can vouch for me as he knows the area." Aakash was glad to see Jai pepped up.

"Yeah, kind of. I, however, was more into the investor network, but this is the entrepreneur network. The energy levels are different here," admitted Vivek.

As they mingled boozing and ogling at women, Aakash bumped into a short guy with an athletic physique.

"I am sorry," apologised Aakash.

"Not a problem man. I am Sahitya. No one notices me because no one can see me coming," replied Sahitya with a smile on his face and a wink.

"Sahitya, that's an interesting name for a person with long hair and stubble," added Aakash as he introduced himself and his friends.

"So what do you do, Sahitya?" Jai was curious.

"I am a wanderer. I keep wandering through people and places and keep recording them," he patted his camera bag to support his point.

"Oh, interesting! My friend Vivek here is also a wanderer," complimented Aakash.

"No wonder his name is Vivek. He needs to wander around to gain wisdom."

Vivek found his comments interesting.

"So...what do you capture?" Vivek asked.

"Just about anything that intrigues me...like this video."

He showed them a compassionate video showing a flock of deer sharing and feeding on plants.

"I was wandering around Jim Corbett National Park. I bet human beings can't do that; they would eat their share and store the rest for their own future."

"That's interesting. So what brings you here?" asked Vivek.

"Creativity!"

Aakash jumped in. "What is so creative about these people?"

"Well, creativity is not just a domain for the artistic field. I have seen a lot of uncreative people there and some very creative people in business."

"You make a good point!" Jai said with exuberance. "I'm in a dead-end job, and this whole entrepreneur speech day has been really inspiring."

"I plan to make some themed videos, and who knows, maybe our paths will cross," Sahitya winked at Jai.

Aakash leaned into Vivek and whispered. "Do you think this Sahitya fellow is gay?"

Vivek shrugged. "What difference does it make to you?" He could hardly complete his sentence when the DJ took over and called out to everyone to join him on stage.

Sathiya waved goodbye and sauntered off.

Aakash and his buddies eagerly participated as the dancing began. Proudy also joined in and received a thunderous roar. He was a Casanova in the literal sense as he smooched a girl while fondling another's breasts, then moved ahead to smack someone's ass as he wrapped his hand around another's waist. The dance floor looked like a small harem of King Proudy.

Aakash was inspired. He flirted with a drunken girl and kissed her gently on the lips as Jai and Vivek watched in amazement. The kiss turned into a smooch as the girl responded positively. He decided to gently slip his hands, not into the top of the girl he was smooching, but the one dancing next to her. Jai and Vivek glanced at each other in shock. The girl turned around, stared at Aakash, gave him a bleak smile and then she slapped him so hard that it took him minutes to realize that the music had stopped and everyone was staring at him.

Jai and Vivek joined Aakash on the dance floor and even though embarrassed by everybody staring at their friend, they laughed their ass off, pointing fingers at him. Soon enough, the stares shifted direction and the trio was kicked out of the party.

Idea!

The journey back in Aakash's car was filled with somber silence, except for a few intermittent bouts of laughter from the two buddies.

Vivek discussed a point, "You have got to give it to him. I mean, what were you thinking? You can't just slip your hand in anyone's top."

"But Proudy can do that?" retorted Aakash.

"What a dog!" remarked Vivek.

"Excuse me, but that girl was fondled by Proudy, but when I tried, she became a *sati savitri*."

"Probably she is loyal to Proudy."

"Give me a break...she is not loyal to anyone. She needs men who can spend on her."

Jai summed up the entire activity in his own words. *"Ek cheez to samajh mein aa gayi. Jis mandir ka prasad khaana ho, ghanti usi ki bajani chahiye."*

Aakash finally laughed with them. By the time they reached home, they were completely exhausted, but light-hearted.

While Aakash and Vivek dozed off immediately, Jai found it difficult to sleep. It seemed the creative talent of the successful entrepreneurs at the seminar had him high strung. He thought about talking to Sneha but it was late. The office events flashed through his mind – his boss' evil face, Gaurav's backstabbing, Sheena's tears and the long and sad faces of the employees who were fired. He decided to call up Sheena the next morning to see how she was coping.

Jai got out of bed and sauntered to the other room, opened the window and gazed at the few stars visible in the polluted sky. It seemed like a perfect metaphor for his office. The silence was intensely calming. Different thoughts popped into his mind. He reflected on them. He recalled what Aakash had said about the lady who had slapped him, whether it had been right or wrong?

The serenity of the night soon turned his mind to tranquil thoughts. It reminded him of his childhood days when he would go to his ancestral place, and sleep next to his grandfather on the terrace. They would talk for hours of the various stars visible in the night sky. It was his Nana who told him that humans were all hanging in space and were just held to the ground due to gravity.

Snap! Jai suddenly felt a strong surge of adrenalin. A sudden realization, a deep instinct hit him that life was about to take a sharp turn. The universe sent signals or probably his dead Nana.

"Idea!" he silently screamed.

He huffed and puffed as his mind expanded the idea: What if people like Sheena and others had a platform where their frustrations could be heard? What if they could speak their mind in public? Unburden themselves. What if there was a platform to vent? Media platforms were inundated with people venting. What they needed was a focused platform. Articles! But, people seldom had time to read. Videos! Yes. People watched and people want to be watched. A platform which allowed for live video recordings of real people and their frustrations. Perfect!

He was so excited, he couldn't contain himself. He rushed to tell Aakash and Vivek. He tried to control his urge to disturb them, but the idea had disturbed him and he wanted to share it with them. The fear of an angry Aakash made him think of an innovative way to keep him cool. He took advantage of the fact that there were no windows in the room and it was as dark during daytime as it appeared at night. He quietly changed the clock time from two a.m. to indicate it was six in the morning, made tea and woke them up.

'Good morning guys! What a lovely morning it is, have some tea," Jai said with enthusiasm.

They found it difficult to open their eyes, but nonetheless managed to wake up, soothed by the idea of being served bed tea.

Aakash glanced at the wall clock. "It's only bloody six!"

"Yeah…I want to discuss some business ideas," Jai said.

"When did you wake up?" Vivek checked with him.

"Oh…I didn't sleep at all."

"What?" The two chorused.

"I had an idea and was thinking about it."

Aakash and Vivek looked surprised that an idea could keep an intoxicated Jai awake.

"It better be as good as your tea." Aakash sipped and gestured at him to go ahead.

"Well, it's about people…common people…common men…common women. Have you guys ever thought abcut how you want the whole world to hear about the injustices commited against you? About life being tough and unfair? I mean, we all have stuff to vent. What if we had a platform to do that?"

"Facebook is one such platform; people keep expressing themselves unnecessarily, overdramatizing everything." Aakash yawned.

"I am talking about videos, where people face the camera and spew, like you can vent about last night's slap. What if I gave you a camera and asked you to say anything you felt like about that girl and the situation, and then upload it on a platform and let people watch it and comment."

The slap's impact was huge and its reference made Aakash contemplate on the idea. But, Vivek had his doubt. "People can do that on YouTube as well. Why would they come to your platform?"

"That's because this would be a specialized platform. All our videos would be themed around rants. Also, we can put advance filters where people can choose to watch or upload their specific kind of rants, be it politics or education or sex. Won't you feel good about it? That there are people willing to listen to you."

"So you want to play agony aunt?" Vivek remarked, blowing into his teacup.

"Not really. We are not qualified for the varied complaints that would crop up. I want people to speak up about their specific issues. And I think it takes guts to speak up. It is probably easy to write just a line or two on social media platform but here, we are talking about facing the camera and making a video. It will make a greater impact. Only a person with some sincerity about his frustration will be able to do that," Jai explained.

Aakash and Vivek were convinced by the logic. It seemed to them like a far-fetched idea, but worth an effort. They continued to discuss the impact of this website if it caught the fancy of the common man – how this could become the voice of the nation, how it would help people focus on ignored problems, the plight of people treated as underdogs.

"I think you guys should do a sample run."Vivek still wasn't convinced, "Get the website registered and try and upload a couple of videos."Vivek clearly indicated that he was not going to participate in this venture.

But the truth was that Vivek did want to vent about his failed marriage. His meditative sessions were losing focus and his own parents were forcing him to sign the divorce papers and give freedom to the poor girl. He had begun to realize that there was something wrong in the way he lived, and to think about it, there was something wrong in the way his parents brought him up. Always a topper, overly disciplined, a loner, non-social, fanatic about studies and his career. His parents were always proud of their over-performing son until he got married. The pressure to perform was tremendous.

Akash looked at his friend in frustration. "You know, the first video I am going to upload would be me cribbing about this spiritual asshole," pointing to Vivek, "not agreeing to do business," Aakash vented.

"I don't want to wash my dirty laundry in public!"Vivek snapped.

"But you do like to read about other people's dirty laundry on Facebook!" Jai retorted pointing to the fact that Vivek still read Aarti's FB status.

"Yes, and I've heard you gossiping about other people's problems," Aakash pointed out. "I mean, you can't be a hypocrite. You do want to vent, but you just want to act high and mighty like you have no problems. You should face it – you are as common as all of us, Vivek."

Vivek looked hurt. The truth would hurt. "You guys are worse than enemies," he said and sighed.

"At least we won't stab you in the back!" Aakash said.

'You've got to face it – this is the way forward; we will be pioneers and if we don't do this, someone else will," Jai said in agitation.

"Okay fine, I will join you on your crazy ride of unburdening online," Vivek said, finally agreeing to be a part of their plan.

The discussion soon returned to the dynamics of business – the team, the kind of videos, the money and the name of the website. Jai suggested making an offer to Sahitya. Aakash and Vivek readily agreed.

Aakash recommended the type of videos. "Let's have categories for different types of frustrations like family, sex, job, money, politics, education, and more ...and let's announce winners with the maximum number of likes every month."

The topic soon turned to the name of the website and revolutionary names like *www.fucktheworld.com*, *www.showthemiddlefinger.com*, *www.makesomenoise.com, www.speakup.com* popped up. Jai finally came up with a suitable name www.ihafa.in, a short form for 'I have a frustrated ass'.

"Sounds like a fucking film award!" Aakash said with excitement. He was wide awake and excited. He rushed out to get a whiteboard. He came back soon enough with the white board and without saying anything, he began to scribble.

"I have written down everything as a checklist so that whenever anyone of us looks at it, he can ponder about the specific points." Aakash said with utmost calm. "What an idea! So, what time is it now?"

Jai suddenly realized that he was caught but kept a straight face. "It's 6.45 a.m."

"Don't tell me the Australian time sweetheart, tell me the IST," Aakash said sarcastically.

"It's 3.30 a.m."

"Good boy! So what do you plan to do now?"

"I don't know, we can have a couple of drinks," suggested Jai.

"And who is going to make eggs?" demanded Aakash in an authoritative tone.

"I will!" Jai said with a broad smile.

Hum Saare Bekaar Karne Chale Vyapaar

Monday morning, Jai returned to work. He found the whole office eerie and lifeless. After the previous night's discussion, he had decided to follow his heart. And Aakash had promised him that he would work out a salary so that he could support his parents. He was relieved that he would be leaving the job soon.

He looked for Gaurav as he passed by his workstation. But he was not at his seat. The office boy said that Gaurav had shifted to Amrit's cabin. He entered. It was time to confront his new boss. Gaurav appeared smug and arrogant. Something about that seat turned normal men into sadists, reflected Jai.

"How was your weekend?" asked Gaurav.

"I don't remember," replied Jai dryly.

"You don't remember?"

"After what happened on Friday,I had to drink so much that I don't remember anything now."

"I guess you are upset about Sheena."

"Her and the four hundred and ninety-nine other people."

"We are helpless, Jai. Come on, let's go down for a smoke."

"I am not in the mood."

Gaurav leaned forward. "Between you and me, your performance is good, how can they fire you?"

"So was Sheena's."

"Sheena had a big attitude problem. The senior management was not happy with her."

"I know what you are talking about, we were all there in the party when a drunk Mallik walked up to her and said 'Quite a feeding you have done with those jugs'."

"People keep flirting all the time in parties," Gaurav tried to cool him down, but there was no point taking the discussion forward.

Jai took his leave. He tried to work, but found it difficult to concentrate. In no time, he was called by Amrit. Gaurav must have been the ass complaining to him. Jai noted that Amrit's cabin was bigger than the previous one and secluded. A monster in his den!

"So how was your weekend?" asked Amrit and then answered it himself. "Lots of booze, eh?"

"Lots of booze and celebration."

"Celebration?"

"For being allowed to continue here."

"Take it as an opportunity. Look at Gaurav, did he tell you that you will be reporting to him now?"

Jai shook his head.

"And don't get upset about others getting fired. Concentrate on your career. Have you heard about Darwin's theory?"

Jai nodded.

"This world is all about the survival of the fittest."

The 'survival of the crookest', rather.

"So are you the fittest, my boy?"

"I am afraid sir, I am not fit today," Jai said with a glum expression. "I feel pukish."

"Then go ahead and puke."

"I have never done that, sir. There are too many rules and conditions. What do you think ?"

"About what?"

"Do you think it is right to puke here in front of you? Whether people should just puke wherever and whenever they feel like? I mean what happens if the urge is high?"

"You want to take a break today?" Amrit asked him, finding his behavior weird.

"That will be great, sir."

Jai headed to the roadside stalls. He ate two plates of bhelpuri – an obsessive habit of eating under stress which he had had from childhood. But, what was the reason behind his stress? Not a job which he had decided to leave? Or was it the insecurity and the unpredictable future?

He wanted to clear his brain. He called up Sheena and met her at a coffee shop. He told her about the office atmosphere and how he had lied to get out of there. She appeared quite relaxed. She was happy to be with her kids and to revisit her hobby in art.

"If only I can tell the world how big these assholes are."

Her frustrations sparked an idea in Jai's mind: *What if Sheena is the first person to upload a video?* It also reassured him that probably they were on the right path. But it was too early for him to reveal it to her. He bid her goodbye and met up with Aakash for lunch. To his surprise, Vivek had skipped his collective meditative session and joined them for a collective beer session. To Vivek's surprise, Jai told him that he had decided to leave his job.

"That's like my boy," encouraged Aakash.

"But, how will you manage?" was Vivek's concern.

"You don't worry about your expenses. We will take care of them," Aakash spoke on behalf of himself and Vivek. Vivek had to oblige.

"For my parents, I will break a fixed deposit. It should keep them well for six months," responded Jai, thinking about what would be his parents' reaction to his decision.

They had put everything they had to make their 'average' son complete his MBA from a prestigious but small town private business school. They were extremely proud, almost in tears when they were invited for 'Family

Day' at his swanky office. "*Ye to foreign jaisa dikhta hai*," said his mother, even though she had never been to any foreign country.

He could never tell his parents that he had left his job and planned to start out on his own unless he could show them that the swanky office they visited belonged to him.

"Great. Let's do it!" Aakash was in top form.

"But, what if this does not work out in six months? Have you consulted your parents?" Vivek prodded Jai.

"I guess I will have to take that risk. And if I consult them, it will never happen."

"I think you should think about it. Take a break from office for some days."

"You took a break from Aarti for more than a year. Were you able to think clearly?" Jai asked Vivek politely. He smiled; a sensitive nerve had been touched.

"I guess you have made up your mind then."

"We are all ready."

Gold Diggers

Jai was, so-to-speak, ill for the entire week as they chalked out the format for the website. Their drawing room became their working office. They created various categories for different kinds of frustrations which included students, working professionals, love, marriage, sex, housewives, politics, etc., to upload their videos. The videos had options of Like or Dislike apart from Comment and Rating. They also planned to create an open forum where people could discuss their frustrations. The process went on for days until they came to their most important feature – Revenues.

"Advertising," said Aakash, emphasizing their most important revenue source.

"And that depends on the viewership," added Vivek.

"Exactly...later on we can also add merchandising, awards events to recognize videos with highest ratings," agreed Aakash.

"Can't we give subscriptions?" queried Jai.

"People won't pay for watching others crib," replied Aakash.

"What about companies?"

"Why would companies pay for it?"

"What if a large number of people want to vent their frustration against one organization? Won't the organization pay us to manage the dent on their brand?" argued Jai.

"That's manipulation," warned Vivek.

"Well, I have seen my targets getting doubled and five hundred people thrown out in less than a week. I am sorry if I feel a bit manipulated," replied Jai sarcastically.

"I understand and we will thrash companies like these, but we should not try to earn from them. It will be like blackmail."

"It won't be blackmail if the companies accept their mistakes and promise to change. Don't you think in such a case we can help them rebrand?"

"I guess so," said Vivek, thoughtful about the idea.

"That's a fantastic idea! Could turn out to be a money spinner," said Aakash excitedly.

"We have to be careful to gauge the intentions of such a company, and that which could be ethically challenging," Vivek added with concern.

They called Sahitya. Luckily, he was in town, and not wandering at faraway places yet. They explained the entire business plan to him. Sahitya was more than excited.

"That's a brilliant idea! People throwing out their frustrations! And what better country to pull it off than ours. A site dedicated just for this will be great."

"And not just any frustration – you can speak against national issues like corruption, inflation, violence, rape; it will be like the voice of this country. Every person will be a news reader reading his news and giving his views," pointed out Aakash.

"Wow! I really look forward to how it evolves," replied Sahitya. "See, I told you there is a lot of creativity in business."

"And this site will cater not only to national issues. Think about teenagers. Even they have gripes. They can come up with anything that bugs their lives."

"Why don't you plan an expert panel to help people resolve their issues?" suggested Sahitya.

"We want it to be a democratic forum, either you can use it to release your frustration or share your problems and wait for the comments from people," replied Vivek.

"But why only videos? What if I do not want to reveal myself?" questioned Sahitya.

"Well in that case you have social media. The whole idea behind this platform is that if you do not have the guts to reveal yourself, you should not have the right to say anything," stated Jai.

"Interesting…so what do you guys want from me?"

"We want someone who is equally enthusiastic and can handle production and editing. Also, someone needs to keep track of the videos getting uploaded to check for any controversial stuff," said Aakash.

"Controversial stuff?"

"Yeah…you never know people may crib intentionally or unintentionally about some politician or celebrity, or worst of all –God."

"Then let them do that, isn't that the whole purpose?"

"But that can land us into legal trouble."

"You are just providing a platform. Just put a disclaimer on the website that people are responsible for their own uploads, we will just keep track that people do not post porn on the site," suggested Sahitya agreeing almost immediately. But, he declined their offer of becoming a partner in the business.

"I am a wanderer. I will do this till the time it excites me and then move on."

They all decided to put their plan into action and shoot some videos. Various names were suggested, including Sheena's. Jai would try to convince her and some other employees fired from the company.

At last Sahitya came up with a name which might be of some help. "Ramakant Trivedi. He is a historian and is quite pissed off with the Archeological Survey of India for not working on excavations as per his findings, and instead listening to a sadhu who dreamt of gold under some fort in UP."

"I read about the historian. Is he the one who was upset with the CM who allowed the digging?" asked Vivek.

"Yeah, that one!" replied Sahitya.

"This can be a good kickstart for us, someone lashing out against the CM," responded Aakash.

Sahitya arranged an appointment with Mr Ramakant Trivedi. Out of the three, Sahitya felt Vivek would have the maturity to convince the senior. They arrived at his residence which was a lonely independent house situated on the outskirts of Delhi.

When they entered his house, they inhaled a strong musty whiff of old paper and archeological finds. It was a special place dedicated to knowledge. Ramakant Trivedi greeted them with polite warmth. With long hair and beard, and dressed in a white kurta-pyjama, he spoke eloquently. He served them special Assam tea. It was the best tea they had ever tasted. Vivek was fascinated by the walls adorned with paintings depicting various rulers of India. The tabletops and every corner of the house were replete with artefacts. In the far corner, a huge cabinet was stuffed with small steel jars with labels on them. Vivek studied each one. Trivedi noticed his enthusiasm.

"Those jars contain the mud of all the excavations I was involved in."

"So, how many are there?" Vivek asked.

"Twenty-four. I was planning to do a silver jubilee around my retirement, but the sadhu had his way."

"Oh! I see...didn't you file a PIL?"

"They are politicians. Do you think they care about PILs?"

Vivek nodded and thought that with their platform, they would have to plan carefully. His excitement for the website increased as he thought about the power it would give to the common man.

"What's your background?" Ramakant asked Vivek. "Sahitya is a self-confessed wanderer."

"Well, I have wandered long enough to be called a non-conformist, but not enough to be called a wanderer," Vivek summarized the past few years of his life.

"So you are an explorer!"

"An explorer who is yet to explore his area of exploration."

Ramakant smiled at his answer. He had admitted his dilemma with such simplicity.

"And what is it that you want from me?"

They explained the entire concept of their online platform.

"While we do not promise any solutions to the problems, we plan to work with the faith that at least your problems will reach a wider audience," finished Vivek.

Ramakant thought for a few moments, then stood up and reached for the steel jars.

"I was thirteen years old when I accompanied my father for my first excavation – of the Harrappa civilization. I was a child with no knowledge but a lot of curiosity. I saw my father inhale and feel the entire dig, he was unlike other archeologists who did it as a job. For him, it was the mission of his life. He was an explorer who believed that life keeps repeating itself and what better way to find out than to dig the historical remains of mankind! You won't believe but their waste disposal mechanism was far better than ours. I picked up my first mud there. I completed my education and was the happiest person on earth when I got selected for the ASI." He offered them more tea.

"What happened after that?" Vivek asked, as he relished the tea.

"You see, I have also tried to live my life as an explorer. I never married, I just kept on exploring. From Ayodhya to Kurukshetra, from Bhagalpuar to Udaipur, I kept researching and living the legacy. There have been times when I was allowed to carry out excavations and times when I was not. Excavation is like madness, you have to be a little mad to start digging a place even on a whim. And mind you, there is no guarantee that anything will ever be discovered, but you still do it because that's what exploration is all about. However, it has never happened because some sadhu of a state of which the political leader is a follower, had a lame dream and now the entire country is debating whether dreams can come true."

The boys looked at the steel jars anew while Ramakant continued. "Your idea is equally mad – you want to dig up on the rationale that people will open up their hearts on your website. You may be right, but it's hard to believe that it can bring about real change. It's like a child who gets a bruise and runs up to his mother and cries in her lap. The most the mother can do is to console him and even though that may be a psychological consolation, the bruise – the pain and suffering – will take its own time to heal."

"I agree, but even if it is just for psychological consolation, every child has a right to tell his story," pointed out Vivek.

"That is true. My father used to say that life is a story and we all are nothing more but stories. The excavations and artefacts have their own stories."

"And you never know if the mother apart from consoling the child also applies an ointment to the bruise," Vivek added smartly.

Ramakant laughed and said, "Well if that ever happens, trust me I will present you with the best ever gift."

"Done!"

•

Aakash, Jai, Vivek and Sahitya planned the contents of their first video with Ramakant Trivedi, the disgruntled archaeologist. They decided to keep the video simple and realistic. Ramakant wanted them to shoot at his home. He wanted to take people through some of the artefacts as he shared his troubles with them. Sahitya arranged for the shooting equipment. Ramakant prepared his speech and the shoot happened within three days of their first meeting. He spoke with poise.

"Namaskaar! My name is Ramakant Trivedi and I am an explorer by choice and an archeologist by profession. I have been fortunate enough to be a part of twenty-four different excavations in a career spanning thirty-five years with the ASI. My stint with the esteemed institution was rewarding as well as satisfying. I thought that I learnt and understood a lot about human psyche as we dug through our excavations." He cleared his throat and continued.

"But I was wrong, for I learnt that the most important thing about the human psyche was a sense of humour. The government and the ASI have money to burn on a whim. Even as I speak, there is a dig happening under a fort in UP because a sadhu dreamed that about a thousand tonnes of gold is buried there. Can you believe it? Educated professionals, archaeologists, researchers and professors are thrown to the sidelines because some sadhu dreamed!" His voice wavered with passion and suppressed anger.

"Yet, I realize that it's an important dig. I mean, imagine if the dream of this sadhu comes true! A thousand tonnes of gold in one dig, isn't that awesome? And what difference does it make if our archeological gold-diggers have stopped other digs? Digs that will help us discover our rich heritage and our ancient culture. Digs that indicate advanced civilization. Seems none of that is important to the ASI. So their funding is to find gold. Yes, a valid investment. It is a business investment. Digs are happening based on ROI," he said sarcastically as he faced the camera.

"These excavations need to be economically sound to continue. I wonder if Shah Jahan was born today and wanted to build the Taj Mahal, would he have gone ahead in the name of love or would he have taken the gold-diggers' route? Hmm, let us calculate the number of Indian and foreign tourists expected each year, multiply that with the ticket price and then see how many years it would take to break-even the construction cost of the Taj Mahal."

He shook his head, as he counted on his fingers. "It is going to take ten years and that's way too long. So the alternate plan – reduce the marble blocks, make it 50% marble and 50% granite and then check. What?! Seven years! Nope, still too long, another plan. Oh sir, you have so many plans? Yes, why not! We are good at planning. Now make just the mausoleum with marble and the rest with granite, what's the break-even now – three years? Fantastic! Let's break even the Taj Mahal cost."

Ramakant spoke with passion about the sad state of the country's archaeological surveys. "I hope a day will come when we will explore for the love of knowledge, for the sake of adventure and to find out the truth of our heritage. Thank you!"

Pull the Curtain or Call the Audience?

The four friends were particularly happy and proud that their first video was from someone of Ramakant's stature. Their dilemma though was about whether they should release the video or wait for more. They were divided on this decision.

"I think we should just launch the video. Let people see it, like it, share it. Let it spread. Then we launch www.ihafa.in," suggested Vivek, recommending a simple start for their platform.

"I think he has a point. Let's make a humble beginning and see to what extent it touches people's nerves," agreed Sahitya.

"I disagree. I think we should give it a proper launch – make a splash," argued Aakash. "I have around fifteen lakhs with me, how much have you got?" he asked Vivek.

"That's not the point. This is a new idea, let's see the initial reactions first."

"Then let's be clear that we are not confident about the idea." Aakash brought the discussion back to square one.

Jai tried a middle path.

"What if we do both together? We launch the site and upload the video on our site and share the link on social media platforms, promote it on free platforms – Facebook, Twitter, blogs – and be prepared with the money.

Once the video starts getting likes, we start spending on the promotion. If it spreads more, we increase the money we put in. If people discard it, we do not spend any money and go back to sharing more videos."

"And how many videos do we plan to share?" Sahitya asked.

"Initially, we need to be careful about the videos we upload, and select those which will attract interest. Once we get traction, we can open it up for anyone to upload while we just do the admin job."

Aakash thought the suggestion was valuable. "Can you believe this young brother of mine is a virgin? He virtually knows everything!"

"You don't have to tell everybody," retorted Jai.

"He is not everybody. He is Sahitya, the future of the past and the past of the future," replied Aakash.

"Speaking of the future, what kind of revenues are we aiming at?" questioned Jai.

"This is going to be a valuation game," replied Aakash.

"Valuation game? Is that a new game in the market?" Jai asked naively, but with a sarcastic tone.

Aakash smiled at Jai. "It's a relatively new game. You earn from the anticipation that your business has the potential to make money. It's typically how a dotcom works. You increase your user base and start earning some revenues, rope in an investor who takes some equity stake and funds the website. The funds in turn further increase the user base which further gets more investors who take equity stakes and bring in some generous dough. This goes on till you – the founder – completely exit out of your own foundations, but not before making a fortune."

"So ultimately the investor earns all the money?"

"Historically, it's the founders and interim investors who have been earning all the money, the final and the real investor seem to be doing just okay."

"So the last man on the island gets stuck, sounds much like the American housing bubble, we don't seem to be learning from our mistakes," Sahitya summed up.

"If we start learning from our mistakes, life won't be that much fun," noted Vivek.

"The best part is that all this happens in a span of three to five years and then you are through…done for the rest of your life," said Aakash.

"But aren't we planning to do this business for the rest of our lives?" Jai asked, concerned.

"We are planning to be entrepreneurs for the rest of our lives, and that does not mean that we stay with the same enterprise. Imagine you are Mr Ramakant. He is an archeologist, but what excitement will he have if he keeps digging the same place all his life? The excitement is in doing twenty-four different excavations. And you know what's the coolest part? It's the first excavation which needs to be logical and rewarding. If you strike gold with the first, then you can be the sleeping sadhu and let the other jokers dig."

They were all revelling in the buzz of excitement of their venture. Jai had planned a resignation that would teach his boss a lesson.

He would make a royal exit from his company, give his boss the arrogant attitude he had been subjected to all this time.

Jai Scares the Dog

Jai had been away from work on the excuse that his nausea had led to food poisoning.

He regretted the fact that he was not a woman, or else he could have declared himself pregnant and taken months off to deliver his baby. He had made up his mind and was determined to go through with the resignation.

As soon as he got to the office, Jai immediately called up Amrit's cabin extension and asked for a meeting.

"Come right now," replied Amrit hanging up the phone and a sudden streak of nervousness gripped Jai's mind.

He hadn't expected Amrit to see him immediately. He thought he would get some time and prepare his opening lines. He gathered courage and decided to face the beast. Better to get it over with. Jai knocked lightly on the door and heard an irritated "Come...Come!"

He entered and saw that the new cabin suited Amrit's personality; hard wood and metal furniture.

Amrit raised his head from behind his monitor and glared. Jai's confidence faltered. "Come on hurry up! Take a seat," said Amrit.

Jai took a seat nervously. "Yes, tell me," Amrit snapped in his usual cold authoritative style.

"I just wanted to say hello," replied Jai hating himself for his cowardice.

"That's good. How are you now?" asked Amrit, giving him a tight fake smile.

"I am fine, thank you," Jai replied and exited with the task of collating a report for North India.

As soon as he reached his cubicle, he received a message from Aakash. 'Did you nail the bastard?' Jai didn't respond.

He tried to work on the report but soon lost interest and headed out to have some tea and smoke. As he sipped and puffed on a cigarette, he could not help but get nostalgic about the time he had spent with Sheena and the not-so-corrupt Gaurav. He called up Sheena and shared that he missed having tea with her. He decided to mention the business idea and his plans of quitting his job. She was genuinely encouraging. Talking to Sheena gave Jai a new zeal of confidence to return to the office and face the beastly boss.

Determined, Jai headed towards Amrit's cabin but just then his mother called. He faltered again, answered the phone and listened to his over-concerned parent as she explained that one of their neighbor's sons left his job to start his own business. She criticized and complained non-stop. Jai deflated like a balloon; all that enthusiasm was gone in a puff. He hung up and was about to return to his cubicle when Amrit, who had noticed him, asked, "All good?"

"The report might get a little delayed. Some IT related problem with my system," Jai justified his stupid hesitation to enter Amrit's cabin.

"Why don't you call the IT guy?" demanded Amrit.

Jai nodded and moved away. He was totally confused about whether he should resign or not. His mother's call had got the better of him. And to make matters worse, Aakash sent another message, 'Is the dog in?' and when Jai replied in the affirmative, 'Then run him over,' was his immediate reply.

Jai thought of stepping out of the office to talk to Aakash but was afraid that he might get shouted at for his cowardice.

Nonetheless, Jai decided to talk to Aakash. He immediately answered the phone arriving straight to the point, "Killed him?"

"Not yet," Jai replied with a feeble voice.

"What happened? I hope you are not afraid of him."

"Not him, but I am scared of my parents."

"What happened to your parents?"

"Nothing happened to them. It's just that I am a good son. The good sons of Indian middle class families get educated and swear to be good employees till the last breath of their work-fuck-ing lives," explained Jai.

Aakash could barely understand, but controlled his exploding temper.

They both watched the dark clouds taking over the sky with thunderous sound effects. Aakash broke the silence. "Do you see dark clouds above you?"

"Yes," replied Jai.

"You know what kind of clouds produce thunderstorms?" Aakash asked further.

"No," replied Jai.

"These clouds which are formed by hot air go through a hell lot of turbulence to finally reach such dramatic heights that nobody can prevent them from causing thunderstorms. That's the process of nature. Do you get it?" explained Aakash completing his rationale really slowly. "This is your nature, buddy. Don't let 'nurture' destroy your 'nature'."

Jai felt like he was stuck in a rut. He pondered on what Aakash had said, and hung up. He gritted his teeth and clenched his fists. He was determined like never before now. He marched forward to Amrit's cabin. Gaurav was also trying to enter at the same time. Jai gave him a hard look and gestured at him to back off. Gaurav was taken aback by Jai's sudden confident stance, and stepped away. Jai did not bother to knock and simply burst in.

Jai announced. "I am leaving!"

"Still not feeling well?" responded Amrit, bewildered.

"I feel awesome. I am leaving the company!" Jai repeated.

There was a pause while the news sunk in. Jai didn't falter or stutter. He stood his ground.

"Where are you going?" asked Amrit.

"I am not changing jobs, I am just leaving this job," Jai stated.

"And what do you intend to do after that?"

"I plan to do my own thing. I am exploring options."

"Tell me some," Amrit had a smirk, his only intention was to ridicule.

Jai didn't explain. Amrit started on the model employee, Gaurav, explained how Gaurav had the potential of making it big, how he understood the senior management and stakeholders.

Jai maintained a stiff silence and waited for Amrit to finish. He simply said.

"Then I am sure I am doing the right thing. With all his knowledge about how, what, when, where and why – in the end Gaurav is going to be just an employee."

He leaned forward and told him about his decision, "On the other hand, *I am going to be an entrepreneur!*"

He did not even wait for Amrit's response and stomped out. It was done. The skies announced through the thunderstorms that the rains burst forth. Jai lit up and took a selfie with a victorious smile on his lips and sent it to Aakash who sent back a selfie with Vivek, cheering with two jugs of beer. And a third jug on the table with the tagline 'Take Me.'

Sanjay Dutt

Jai and Sneha met at Dilli Haat. She had decided to meet him only if he took her to a livelier place. Dilli Haat was an open exhibition of cultural items from across the country with different stalls allocated to different states. For girls, it was mostly about shopping, eating Chinese food, and getting mehendi applied on their hands. For guys, this was the best place as the girls never wanted to leave early.

As they strolled through the place, Sneha surveyed the various stalls. Jai wanted to share his experience of what happened in the past few days, but she was too preoccupied. It took him a while to figure out that she might be angry. He offered to buy something nice for her, but she coldly refused, "I can buy what I want by myself."

Her anger was out of the bag now and she moved to the next stall. He followed her, gathered his courage and clasped her hand. But when she gave him a surprised look, he let go. She gave him a cute smile and offered her hand.

Jai froze. Time seemed to have stopped and sounds faded, as they were lost in each other. All her anger disappeared when she noticed that he was blushing more than her and his ears had turned red.

"You are such a girl!Look at your ears."

His ears felt hot to the touch.

"That's because it's cold outside," Jai said trying to hide his embarrassment.

"Do you want to feel warm?"

"How?" Jai asked.

She came close to him and whispered, "Do you want a hug?"

"Here?" Jai asked feeling both happy and concerned about the offer as he looked at the passers-by.

"It's a one time offer, think about it while I get my hands decorated with mehendi."

He was lost in his thoughts as Sneha checked out the designs from the catalogue and took a seat. He followed and sat next to her.

"It will be weird…I mean doing it here," Jai expressed his concern.

"You know what's weird? Not meeting or talking for ten whole days, that's weird…giving cold replies to messages, that's weird."

Sneha returned to her angry avatar.

"It's my mistake. But I was confused, I wanted to tell you once I was sure about it."

"Why? Don't you think we can share our confusions with each other?"

"Sure we can!"

"Then help me with the designs!" He glanced through the catalogue

He picked a design which required a guy's name to be included in it. The mehendi artist held Sneha's hand and started his intricate artwork.

"So, you all charged up about the business?"

He took her through the website idea as she laughed uncontrollably.

The mehendi artist requested her not to move.

"You really think people will post their videos?" she asked Jai.

"Why? Do you think they won't?"

"I don't know. People are generally very shy. They can't even hug openly," Sneha said slyly.

"They can. It's just that it does not look good."

"How can two people hugging each other not look good? Have you watched the film *Munnabhai MBBS*?"

"Ample times."

"Didn't you learn anything from it?"

"So, basically a friendly hug?"

"A *warm* friendly hug."

"I think we can do that."

He leaned slowly towards her and managed a warm hug. Their bodies met for the first time and it felt like bliss. When the mehendi artist asked her for her other hand, they had to separate.

For the next couple of minutes, they were silent, lost in their new-found heaven, glancing around, sharing awkward smiles. The rouge hue of his ears had now spread across his face. The mehendi artist was just about to finish his artwork, when he asked Sneha what name she wanted on her hand. Sneha glanced at Jai and wondered whether his rosiness would spread all over his body if she mentioned his name.

"Sanjay Dutt!" Sneha said. Jai was so shocked, the colour drained from his face.

"You look fine now."

"What do you mean?" demanded Jai.

She turned back at the mehendi artist and said, "Bhaiya, the name is Jai."

Search for the Stars

The business started to take shape and so did their office. Their drawing room was converted into a workplace. The worn-out sofas were replaced with basic infrastructure – tables, chairs and a white board. They made it a point to reach their office by nine – a journey which took less than five seconds, except for Sahitya, who travelled an hour every day. However, the only guy to reach office late was Aakash who somehow managed to wake up at nine, make general conversations with the other three partners and then slip to his room to get ready.

Once settled in their new office, they made a list of their key requirements – right from technology to driving traffic to managing content on their platform to finances and most importantly - videos.

"We need outstanding videos!" reiterated Aakash for the umpteenth time.

"We already have one outstanding video. Let the website go live and make it viral," insisted Vivek, still holding ground that they should take it one step at a time.

"We should not open the site with just one video," argued Aakash.

"I agree. We should have at least five videos to start with and a mechanism so that we can add more at regular intervals," suggested Jai.

"Exactly, we have to hit it properly. Any update from Sheena?"

"She hasn't made up her mind yet," Jai said. Aakash was irritated. Sheena had stopped taking Jai's calls after he made the offer. Jai realized that her non-responsive attitude could be a personal reason – she was after all a wife and a mother of two kids. But, he did not want to tell Akash the truth.

But typical of Aakash, he had to vent. "Pompous woman! We are giving her the platform and she's acting like some glamour queen. "

Vivek noted Jai's face turning pale and intervened. "See, a lot of people are going to back out, especially since it's a new idea. We have to approach more people from different walks of life."

"I agree. Let me figure out some more interesting people like Mr Trivedi," added Sahitya.

"I think we should just get out of the office and try and meet as many people as we can," suggested Aakash and the entire team agreed almost immediately.

They decided to split up in pairs.

"I will go with Sahitya," declared Vivek and guided Jai aside, "You go with this guy," he said and pointed a finger at Aakash.

"What do you mean this guy?" Aakash retorted strongly.

"I have a rapport with Sahitya, we went to meet Mr Trivedi together," Vivek explained calmly.

"Fair enough, even though you did not answer my 'this guy' question."

The team split up and Jai left with Aakash in his car. They drove slowly through the roads trying to figure out who would be interesting. They discussed people ranging from politicians, social workers, corporate executives, students, angry housewives and down to the street sleepers. As they waited in their car for the red light to turn green, they noticed street kids begging and their parents resting on the footpath under a flyover.

"Who else can be more frustrated than these people?" Aakash said excitedly. They decided to meet them.

The homeless people's home constituted of a small tent where the man of the house was fast asleep. The woman was cooking on a crude chulha, fuelled by wood taken from broken branches of trees. The grandparents smoked small butts of cigarettes thrown away by smokers. Aakash and Jai reached their small world and explained their video. The sleepy beggar was irritated by this disturbance, but listened to their intense animated agenda with a bored expression.

"Humein kya karna hoga?" asked the man.

"Aapko apne dil ki baat bolni hai...samaaj ko lekar, sarkaar ko lekar, apne jeevan ko lekar...bejijhak," responded Aakash.

"Hum kuch bhi bol sakte hain?"

"Ji...kuch bhi."

"Aur hum bol ke phas gaye to?"

"Ji aap phasenge kyun?"

"Kyun nahi phas sakte? Itni muskil se to yahan ghar banaye hain pulsion ko khila-khila ke...haraami her hafte paisa leke jaate hain...tumhaari pichchar dekh kar humko yahan se hata diya to kaun jimmevaari lega?"

"Aapko yahan se koi nahin hatayega, balki aapki baat sab tak pahunchegi," explained Jai trying to convince him.

"Aap newswaale ho kya?"

Aakash tried to explain the internet platform where his video would be viewed. He tried to convince the man that the video would be watched all over the globe. But the man had an expression as if he had spotted a UFO. Just then the kids returned from their begging duties. They gave their father the money. One of his sons held out a half-eaten burger as part of the alms. All the kids looked at their father with expectation, wondering who would get the branded burger. The man thought for a while and passed on the burger to his youngest daughter saying that it was her turn. The girl grabbed the burger and jumped with excitement rushing towards her mother giving her a bite as well. The father was proud of his decision and turned towards Aakash and Jai to boast, *"Ladke-ladki mein koi farak nahi rakhte hum."* Aakash and Jai responded with warm smiles as Aakash played his card and replied, *"Hum to chahte hain ki duniya mein kisi ke beech koi farak nahi ho."*

The man thought about their idea and dragged one of his sons to a corner to understand this internet. The kid who had just reached adolescence explained the way some of his privileged friends had told him. The man looked at Aakash and Jai furiously. He picked up a small stone to scare them away.

"Bhago yahan se, behanchod!" he shouted at them. They were shocked at his sudden outburst.

"Magar hua kya?" demanded Aakash.

"Humko kya chutiya samajhte ho? Humko sab pata chal gaya hai...humari nangi pichchar dikhayoge logon ko!"

"Kisne kaha ye aapse?" asked Aakash, horrified.

"Hum sadak pe rehte hain iska matlab ye nahi ki humein kuch pata nahi hai."

"Hum aisa kuch nahi karne waale...aap jin kapdon mein hain, unhi kapdon mein pichchar banayenge."

"Phir chutiya kaat rahe ho...humko pata hai tum baad mein humare kapde utar doge...arre sab kuch hota hai aaj kal saali maseen par."

Jai whispered to Aakash that he was referring to morphing. But before he could respond to the man, his mother called and scolded him. She then explained something which he understood pretty well, evident from his confident and happy face. He returned with his mother following him.

"Ek sarat pe karenge tumhaari pichchar," the man said with a heightened tone of voice.

Aakash and Jai looked at him eagerly.

"Do hajaar rupay lagenge."

Aakash was glad that the man was convinced enough to negotiate. He made a counter offer of five hundred bucks but the man stuck to his figure. Aakash increased the amount to seven hundred fifty when the man's mother responded with a fifteen hundred. Aakash made a final offer of a thousand and the deal was sealed.

"Lekin aapko khul ke bolna hoga," Aakash said.

"Gaand phaad bolenge...tum le to aayo apna camera!" declared the mother while her son smiled proudly at her for supporting him.

Aakash and Jai looked at each other in shock and told them that they will be back in a few days with the camera. When they were about to leave, the man demanded half advance. A hesitant Aakash glanced at the mother who nodded at him as he took out a five-hundred-rupee-note from his wallet.

•

After their first victory, Aakash suggested to Jai that they go to what he considered the second most frustrated place on earth – colleges.

"No one is frustrated during college life," said Jai trying to understand his point of view as Aakash parked his car in the campus.

"You bet they are. College life is the time you don't know whether you are happy or frustrated because you are hormonal."

"So, overexcited people can be good for our business?"

"Exactly! Now let's go and talk to the principal or somebody senior."

"Wait…wait…do you think the principal is going to let them participate in www.ihafa.in?"

"Don't worry…we won't tell them the full form."

"But we don't need them. Let's just talk to some students here," said Jai.

They approached some students standing in the park, introduced themselves and their website. This would be an opportunity for students to spill their guts, whatever they wanted to say through the medium of videos. A huge crowd gathered in the park as they stood on a small pavement telling them about the website and kind of videos. Once they finished, they asked the students. "Which one of you would like to participate?" and almost all of them raised their hands.

Aakash and Jai exchanged glances with pride and welcomed the students to prepare for an audition soon.

•

Vivek and Sahitya discussed their options which were different from the ones planned by Aakash and Jai. They pondered over divorce cases, rape victims, orphans, social activists, when Sahitya came up with the option of a settlement home for eunuchs. Sahitya knew the manager of the home which they could go visit. Vivek was hesitant going to a place full of eunuchs and addressed his concern in the lamest way possible:

"Is it safe?"

Sahitya understood that his point of view came from his observation of eunuchs at marriage ceremonies, trains, traffic lights and other places where they resorted to vulgar means to collect money from people. He explained that the reason why eunuchs have to resort to such tactics is due to their inacceptance by society. He decided that both of them should pay a visit to the settlement home.

They reached the location and Sahitya introduced Vivek to the manager who was also a eunuch. They strolled around the area and the working facility where products were handmade. Sahitya explained the purpose of their website and asked if anyone would volunteer for their video. The manager thought for a while and decided to call Tabassum. While Tabassum was on her way, the manager mentioned that she belonged to a good Muslim family and had just finished her school.

"She was always a good student and planned to become a doctor before the society discovered that she was not normal. Her family refused to accept the society's ostracization and treated their daughter well. But the non-acceptance of eunuchs was so strong in the society that the family had to succumb to societal pressure to let Tabassum go. She now teaches science and makes handicrafts at the center," he explained.

A beautiful girl in the prime of her youth entered the manager's cabin and introduced herself as Tabassum. She shook hands with Sahitya and Vivek. They were overwhelmed by her beauty and simplicity. She agreed to the video with a smile. They planned a date for the shoot.

As Sahitya and Vivek drove away they were lost in thought, trying to fathom the harsh life of Tabassum and millions of others. And they believed that by giving voice to people like Tabassum, they could create a change in attitude in the country.

But, was their platform going to bring a transformation or would it add to more nuisance? Only time would tell.

Roll Camera, Action!

In the evening, they all gathered at their office and listed out their probable videos:

Archaeologist

Man on the street

Tabassum

College students

Over the next few days, they continued to meet various people from all walks of life – housewives, teachers, bureaucrats, party workers, youth, sex workers, corporate executives, laborers, religious pundits, divorcees, army officers, college students and even more college students.

They finally decided the dates and timings for shooting the various videos and the day came when it was time to roll.

Man on the Street

They shot the video depicting his family, his outdoor dilapidated home and of course his street address. The filming continued while the man spoke facing the camera.

"Pichle hafte jab hum apne kamre mein dopahar ki neend poori kar rahe the, to ye do launde humare paas aaye aur bole ki humein aapki pichchar banani hai. Humne kaha bhaisaab hum koi Khan to hain nahin, to humari pichchar kaun dekhega. Inhone jawaab diya ki pichchar poori duniya dekhegi. Arre bhai hum garib hain, chutiye nahi. Lekin humne vaada kiya aur hum koi neta bhi nahi hain

jo vaada karke mukar jayein to aaj hum yahan khade hain aap sabke saamne…" He cleared his throat before he continued.

"Humara janam isi sahar apni Dilli mein Karol Bagh ke ek footpath pe hua tha. Kuch bees saal ki umar tak humne Karol Bagh ke alava Dilli ki koi jagah nahi dekhi, lekin humne duniya bahut dekhi wahan footpath par. Phir humari saadi hui aur humari jindagi mein phocus aaya. Humne bahut mehnat ki aur dheere dheere footpath badalte badalte hum yahan tak pahunche. Ab hum bhi kehte hain ki hum South Dilli waale ho gaye hain." He smiled proudly.

"Lekin iska matlab ye nahi ki hum khus hain, humari bahut sikayatein *hain sarkaar se. Pehle to ye ki policewaalon ki itni jaldi badli na ki jaye, behanchod itni muskil se to ek ke saath rate phix hota hai ki doosra harami aa jaata hai. Doosri ye ki kam se kam ladiz ke liye ek snan-ghar banaya jaye. Humari joru jab nahane jaati hai to doosre footpath ke haraami launde ass-paas mandarate rehte hain. Aur teesri aur sabse jaroori, itne log raat ko footpath pe rehte hain ki inke manoranjan ke liye her footpath pe ek TV hona chahiye, nahi to saala manoranjan ke naam pe haal hi mein humara chhatvan bachcha hone ja raha hai. Kab tak yahi manoranjan karenge hum, in haraamkhoron ko paanch saal ki umar se pehle bheekh maangane bhi to nahi bhej sakte."* He sighed heavily.

"Ab hum vida lete hain. Humse Jai Hind bolne ki ummeed mat rakhna, kyunki saala Jai to Solay mein gujar gaya to Hind akela kya karega??"

Aakash and Jai were proud of this fellow and the ease with which he spoke. They paid him the remaining money and moved on.

Next on the list was Tabassum. The girl faced the camera confidently. She smiled throughout the shoot, even though her eyes told a different story.

Tabassum – The Weeping Girl with a Smile

"Hello. My name is Tabassum Khan and I am not a terrorist (smiles). Sorry, it was just a bad joke because I actually feel that I am worse than a terrorist…I am a eunuch. Terrorists are lucky fellows; they plan and they kill. But even when they do so, everybody wants them. The government wants to catch them, put them into prison, may be rehabilitate them so that they can live a normal life in the society. But in our case, the same society discards us, throws us away and the non-support of government converts us into cultural terrorists. I guess it's a big price we pay for non-performance of sex and reproduction. I was always a good student. I wanted to be a doctor, and even though I am capable to compete for a seat, I cannot compete with the big question – Sex: Male or Female?" She took a deep breath and continued.

"I won't make this more melodramatic. My parents are already shattered. As a child, I remember the heading of a chapter I read in our Moral Science class – 'Man is a social animal'. I think the heading should be changed to 'Man is a sexual animal'. Thank you!"

There was heaviness in the air; many were emotional as Tabassum rushed off to her room, unable to control her tears. Vivek asked the Centre Manager if they could offer some help in any way so that she could fulfill her dream of studying medicine. The manager replied that they had already written to the Education Minister and were awaiting a response.

With a heavy heart, they moved to the next video on their list. They arrived at the studio where the students had gathered for the auditions. There was a long queue already waiting. There were more than two hundred and fifty eager students and more were joining in.

Surprised at this amazing turnout, they would need time to figure out the right one. The studio assistant asked them to start the auditions immediately. They started the process, calling the participants one by one. Barring a few students who actually cribbed about studies and the curriculum, all the others sounded like clones. They complained about college discipline, banning of miniskirts, lack of open book examinations, and the silliest was the inflexible canteen timings and the need for more concerts.

The auditions kept them awake late into the night and continued the next day all throughout the afternoon when they finally hit the jackpot. A Bengali girl, plump and cute, dressed in a short skirt faced the camera. She exuded so much casual confidence that the cameraman was lost in her charm.

Bengali Beauty – Heavy Duty

"Hello ma frenz, ma family, ma doggie Coo-chee-coo me loves ya coochee & ma countrymen. Me don wanna sound like a cribster. U know…dats jus not me…so me jus gonna tell ya some of ma thots…wot me feels wot me thinks…d other day me went to a bar wid ma friendz in d afternoon…it was hot and v felt v shld hv beer…but d moment v were abot to enter d bar, me saw gals beggin on d street…and me felt bad…very bad…so me went into d bar and got beer for her begga frenz…ma frenz and da bar guys were laufing at me but me dint care…everybody gives dem money and food but me…me gave dem an experience de will never forget…dats wot me is all abot…experience." She smiled seductively.

"Me got to tell ya dat me don like her college dean…he don want d college to progress…he banned wearing mini skirts for gals in college…me felt bad…very bad…coz ven me wore mini skirts, all d oder gals felt jealous and copied me and d fashion status of d entire college went up…but me dint care…dats wot me is all abot…raising d bar." She grinned.

"Me also din like ven college bannedYoYo Honey Singh's performance in d college…me says first listen to his songs…d lyrics…me is gonna sing for ya guys to explain better…

"Aina vi na dope-shope marya karo…khaali pet liver na sadiya karo…YoYo Honey Singh…

"Got it…d guy is givin social message thru his songs…dats wot the gar-ment also wants…less booze, less smoke, less dope…but d college don understand…me felt bad…very bad…but me dint care…dats wot me is all abot…me don give a fuck." She showed her middle finger.

"Me thinks me has said a lot…but before me goes, me is jus gonna tell u the one beautiful rule for an amazing time on this planet…u jus need to take three things lightly…jus three things and me promises u dat ur life would be beautiful…those three things are God, Money and Death…trust me…take these things lightly and feel the difference…these are d only things dat makes ur life heavy…people say to find a purpose in ur life…me says stop looking for a purpose…jus be me…now, its time for me to go…c ya!" She wiggled her fingers.

They were over the moon, and could not thank her enough for her quirky wisdom. Their purpose was served and they discontinued further auditions. The students were informed that they could shoot and upload videos once the site was up and running.

•

They gathered once again at their office to discuss the launch. They now had four videos ready and in addition they could add a sex worker cribbing that people still didn't wear condoms, or a junior political party worker complaining that they were asked to be careful of the media. But, the team was still not convinced about the two videos and debated heavily on whether they should wait, or just get started with the four. In the middle of their discussions, they were interrupted by the door bell. Jai jumped up to get it. Aakash, Vivek and Sahitya were surprised at his sudden energy when all through the discussion Jai had been silent. He returned with a pen drive and fed it into the laptop.

Sheena's Sensation

A fierce looking Sheena stares at the camera and bursts out confidently.

"Hi! My name is Sheena Malik and I worked for a company called Best Mobile Technologies for four years before I was fired recently. I was told that the reason for my unexpected exit was not my non-performance but the non-performance of the company due to tough economic conditions. While I was mature and professional, and made a peaceful exit out of my office, I have some questions...no sorry...some BASIC questions for the senior staff of BMT. 1) What exactly do you mean when you say non-performance due to tough economic conditions – is it due to the fact that India as a market is now fucked-up or because you as Strategists fucked up? 2.) Why was a revised target of three crores given to me just twenty days before I was fired when my previous target was just 1.20 crores – did you really believe in me as a performer when you revised my target or were you trying to mock me? 3.) Why were people who were hired just six months ago, fired so soon – were they such assholes that they needed firing or were the seniors such assholes to recruit such staff in the first place? 4.) Why is it that even after the non-performance of the company, most of the staff that got fired was below managerial level and only a couple of senior management guys bore the brunt?" she huffed.

"There are several more questions but I think these are enough to shake the weak asses of BMT's senior management. In a way it's good for me as I have two kids to take care of. But it's pathetic to see people who are struggling to make ends meet suddenly kicked out. I hope some senior jokers experience this struggle so that they can realize what it is like to suffer because of fucked-up decisions made at the corporate level." She smiled coldly.

"And before I wrap up, I want to give out a message to one of the senior-most MCP in the system who told me in a party that I have big jugs. The drunkard knows who I am referring to. Yes, I have big boobs, you son of a bitch! I have big boobs which you kept talking to, and you know why...because I am a mother of two kids who were properly fed on my milk. I doubt your mother ever fed you with hers!"

The video ended with that startling revelation. Jai and Sahitya were grinning ear to ear, while Aakash and Vivek were in shock.

"That was something!" exclaimed Aakash.

"Why didn't you tell me about this?" Vivek demanded from Jai.

"You go with this guy!" Jai said sarcastically reminding him that he had sent him with Aakash.

"But, how did you pull this off?" asked Aakash.

"I sent her an emotional message and she agreed."

"You black-mailed her emotionally! Fantastic!" cried out Aakash, pulling Jai's cheeks.

"But don't you think she can be sued by the company for speaking so strongly?" intervened Sahitya.

"She can, but she was smart enough to talk about that sexual derogatory remark as the grand finale. So if they decide to sue her, she can counter sue and ruin their reputation completely." Vivek smiled.

"Sheena made a smart move! She has the boobs and the brains," Aakash said while everyone glared at him.

The Current Account Party

The website had a spunky display, mostly in shades of blues and greys. It gave a modern look. They uploaded the videos and launched the website the very next morning.

Over the next month, they spent their hours updating friends and uploading video links on various social media platforms. Their weekly target of uploading two videos was replaced by four; many viewers, especially the youth, were attracted to the website. Sheena was a clear winner with more than 200,000 hits in one month, followed by the Bengali beauty video with 125,000 hits. No one was really bothered about the Man on the Street. Tabassum's video received less hits, but more comments. The archaeologist's video was the lowest viewed, with only 10,000 hits. He wondered if he should have shown some more of his personal artefact collections. *Yes, if they were sculptures of naked women,* Aakash thought snidely.

While they celebrated the increase in visitor views on their website, they were equally concerned whether to open up the website for people to upload videos on their own. The maximum growth could only be achieved by making it the people's platform. But, it needed investment – a large amount they could not pull off on their own. They needed to pitch the website to investors, but investors would ask for current revenues.

Sheena's video helped their cause through advertising revenue from an online advertising agency which paid them fifty thousand rupees to run fifteen second adverts of one of their clients which dealt in making plus-sized lingerie, also appointing her as one of the brand ambassadors owing to her gaining popularity in the corporate circles.

Happy with the development, the three entrepreneurs invited Sheena and her husband for dinner to an upmarket Italian restaurant. Her husband, Nakul, was extremely pumped up about their website idea but hardly got a word edgewise as Sheena was a nonstop chatter-box. She was thrilled to be the brand ambassador of the lingerie brand- surprising moments of fame. She nararated her visit to the lingerie brand office. They praised her for her courageous video and signed her on. She couldn't stop chuckling with excitement.

Aakash asked, "So, how did you guys meet?"

Both Nakul and Sheena blushed. Sheena continued chuckling as she told them.

"Since we were kids, we stayed in the same locality and we met for the first time during a Mata ka Jagran. I played Mata and was made to sit on a tiger. His elder brother played the tiger, whereas he played the devil. I fell for him the moment I killed this small little devil with my *trishul*. And he fell for me; at least that's what he told me later. But years went by and he never proposed. So, I started going around with other guys, making this poor guy feel jealous. Then one day, he finally behaved like a man and proposed to me. We were all playing this game called Raja, Mantri, Chor, Sipahi – it is played with paper strips which you need to open and find out who you are. So, he marked a strip slightly black, and no one was supposed to pick it up as it was marked for me, and guess what happened? I had no option but to pick that strip and the moment I opened it...well, it obviously had Chor written on it with a small heart with this little devil's name in it!" She giggled.

"Oh God! That's so romantic," Aakash humoured them.

"Isn't it? I just fell for him," continued Sheena, oblivious to his cynicism. As far as Nakul was concerned, the poor guy was blushing. Sheena pulled his ear to show it to them. Jai was embarrassed for the guy.

"Surely my friend has a lot of blood in him," Aakash smiled at Nakul.

Jai changed the subject to save the poor chap. "So, you are a banker?"

"Yes. Not as exciting as your work, but it brings in the dough," replied Nakul.

"Can you help us open up a current account?" asked Jai knowing that they had their first cheque but did not have an account to park the money.

"Do you have a registered company?"

"Yeah. It's called IHAFA Pvt. Ltd."

"Then it shouldn't take much time. Come to the bank tomorrow and I will open your account."

•

The next day, Aakash was eager to get to the bank. To everyone's surprise, he woke up unusually early, got dressed and was out the door by 9.30 a.m. Nakul helped him handle all the paper work, and within the same day IHAFA Pvt. Ltd. had an official bank account. Aakash immediately deposited their first cheque.

When Aakash returned he was on top of the world, "We've got to have a Current Account Party!"

Jai looked glum, "Not another one of your wild parties."

"Some beer and kebabs," Vivek taunted, thumping Jai on the back, causing him to stumble.

Aakash shook his head, "You guys are such geeks. We are having a pool party at a farmhouse. So be there tomorrow, okay!"

Vivek and Jai exchanged glances, not one of those crazy parties again. "Shit!"

The next day, Jai and Vivek arrived at the farmhouse. Aakash and many of his friends were there already, splashing around in the pool, most of them looking super fit and supercool in their swimming gear. Aakash was by the bar, chatting up a curvaceous female in a bikini.

Vivek and Jai sidled up to the bar and waved to Aakash. The girl picked up her cocktail and whispered to Aakash winking at him before she left. As she sauntered to the pool, male eyes followed her every move.

"Why the fuck are you guys late?" Aakash hissed, snapping his friends out of their hypnotic state.

Vivek looked upset. "First you tell us, who are all these people?"

"These are all my friends," exclaimed Aakash.

"Since when do you have these many friends?" Jai asked.

"Oh come on! The more the merrier!" Aakash said lightly.

"No my friend," Vivek said softly, "the less the merrier." He directed his friend's attention to the pool.

Aakash asked, "It's a pool party, what did you expect them to wear? " Then he noticed his friends' attires.

Jai smiled snidely. "We don't have pool shorts or pool type bodies."

"Yes, I figured!" Aakash said, "I have kept some shorts for you guys. Go get them, they are behind the bar."

"Crap!" Jai muttered.

"I don't know these people. I thought you would invite some common friends," Vivek whined.

"But we don't have any common friends," Aakash said coolly.

"What about Sahitya?"

"Look!" Aakash pointed. "He's in the pool." They noticed he was relaxed with a beer and chatting up with a girl.

"See, he's such a good sport," Aakash waved at him. "Also, there's Nakul."

"So you invited Nakul and Sheena?" Jai asked.

"Nope. Just Nakul."

Jai freaked out. "Are you out of your mind?! *You invited Nakul without Sheena?*"

"Why? You wanted to see the booby-licious lady in a bikini?"

"Behave yourself," Jai said acidly.

Aakash grinned. "Okay sorry, but definitely bubbly-licious! I mean she is so bubbly, chirpy, talkative that she doesn't let the poor hubby speak. I invited him so that he could have a free conversation with someone."

Jai was appeased. "Where is he?"

Aakash pointed at a man standing in one corner of the pool, looking as red as a king prawn.

"Look at the poor red chap! I think you guys should give him company."

"But I don't know how to swim," Jai exclaimed.

Aakash patted him like he was a kid. "My dear friend, the entire pool is just five feet in depth, you will not drown."

Aakash picked up his beer and was about to head towards the pool.

"Wait…first tell me, how much money have we splurged on this party?" Vivek asked.

Aakash looked at him with a cool expression. "Just relax, this place and the pool belongs to a dear friend. We just pitched in for food and drinks."

"Oh! That's good," Jai said.

Vivek still wanted his answer. "So, how much?"

"Only twenty thousand bucks."

"That's a lot! We have just fifty thousand in our current account. I mean, we should have saved it." Jai said. "Get some interest on it."

Aakash wasn't looking troubled at all. In fact, he was gazing out at the crowd having fun at the poolside. "Calm down, you guys are always overreacting like girls. I spoke to the ad agency yesterday, we have another brand lined up, so don't worry about revenue. Besides, you don't get any interest on funds in current accounts."

"Huh?" Jai looked confused.

Aakash turned to Vivek. "Please explain it to him. I've got to check out that chick.

Aakash headed towards the pool. He cracked a joke, and all the girls giggled. He jumped in, splashing water over a girl as she playfully called him naughty. Jai watched Aakash from a distance.

"This guy really knows how to get women's attention."

"He is a natural," Vivek commented and took a sip from his beer. "Anyway, banks never pay interest on the current account; they just maintain the balances with them and call it float."

"Float?"

"Float for liquidity."

"Float on our money?"

"Yeah."

"What do they do with our money?"

"They lend it out and earn interest. They call it spread."

"Is this some kind of swimming lesson? Float and spread! If they earn interest, why don't they pay it to us?" Jai stared incredulously.

"That's how the banking industry works." Vivek was watching the boisterous play in the pool.

They noticed Nakul doing a back float. He seemed happy in his own space.

"Looks like he is having a nice time all by himself," Vivek commented.

The two then went behind the bar and changed into shorts. Before they could get into the pool, Jai filled up a shot glass with neat scotch and gulped it.

"Easy. We have the entire day ahead of us," Vivek warned.

"Nothing like that, I just need to get drunk otherwise I will feel shy in the pool," Jai said.

"Hmm...you have a good point."

Vivek left his half glass of beer and joined Jai with gulps of a large peg of scotch. They decided to enter the pool together for moral support. They were conscious of their half-naked state. Nakul welcomed them into the pool. Jai was in a taunting mood after the newly discovered knowledge of current accounts.

"So you floating well, my friend?" Jai said to Nakul.

"Pretty much...I noticed if you spread your arms, you float better."

"Why not? Your arms are spread and red."

Nakul smiled embarrassedly at his sun burned arms, chest and belly.

"I guess Aakash was right. I do have a lot of blood in me," he snickered.

Aakash headed towards them. But, on the way noticed a girl spluttering, and saved her from drowning for which he received a peck on his cheek. He winked at Jai and gestured he should move towards the girls clinging to the edge; they didn't know how to swim.

"How are my friends doing?"

"Your friends can only feel fantastic," Nakul exclaimed. Aakash laughed.

By the poolside, they munched contentedly on tikkas when a spunky female jumped into the pool, causing water to splash all over the food.

Aakash smiled. "Hey Tina, enough splashing! Let my friends eat!"

"Sorry, but tell me what's this party about?" Tina giggled.

"I started this website with my friends. Guess what! We got our first cheque and we opened our own current account."

"Oh my God! You are a rockstar," Tina squealed.

She clambered on him and gave him a tight hug as they slid towards a corner to chat. Nakul glided towards Jai and Vivek.

"Please explain something," Nakul started. "I open current accounts all day but I don't get this kind of female reaction."

"His current account openings are very different. Firstly, his accounts have a lot of current in them and secondly, they open both sides," Vivek snickered.

Nakul glanced at Vivek. "Lucky fellow."

Jai watched Aakash as he easily mingled with girls, hugging and kissing them, sometimes patting them on their bottoms. Jai plucked up courage and decided to be like Aakash. He gestured to an attendant to get him a bottle of scotch. Without anyone noticing, he drank more than half of it. He noticed his first target and reached for her taking giant steps. The booze had done its job and he wasn't nervous at all. He reached her and smiled.

"Hi! My name is Jai, I'm Aakash's friend."

She gave him a smile.

"Who is Aakash?"

Her question disappointed him and he bid her goodbye.

"What the fuck is this?" Jai smarted and stumbled upon Aakash.

"What happened?" Aakash asked.

"That girl doesn't know you."

"Oh that one, she is with a friend of mine. You hit on her?"

"Tried and was highly embarrassed," Jai said.

"Don't be. You know the reason why Casanova was Casanova? He never stopped trying."

"What do you mean?" Jai asked.

"See, I don't get all the girls I want. There is always a 60-70% rejection ratio, but the idea is that if you try for ten, you'll easily get three."

"That's quite motivating! I should get going. I have a target for myself today."

"How many?"

"Five!"

"Easy peasy," Aakash winked.

Jai noticed a skinny but attractive girl by the edge of the pool, drinking wine and reading a book. The book was getting wet with the occasional splashes of water, but she didn't seem to mind. He introduced himself.

"Hi...my name is Jai. Aakash is my partner."

"Hi Jai! Congrats for the current account."

The girl gave him a tight hug.

"Thanks...I see your book is getting all wet."

"Yeah! I love reading wet pages, I like the texture."

He watched her touching the wet page with her palm and felt his excitement in the warmth of his ear.

"Are my ears red?"

"Completely!"

His red ears reminded him of Sneha and he bade her goodbye. He fell into the ethical dilemma of being loyal to Sneha and yet wanting to reach his personal target of flirting with five girls. He spent the next ten minutes in the centre of the pool evaluating and finally decided to go for it.

He glided towards various girls introducing himself as Aakash's partner, or the founder of www.ihafa.in, or the guy who had thrown the current account party, and received his share of hugs and kisses. By the time he completed his target, he was like a red replica of Nakul. He returned to his friends.

"How did it go?"Vivek asked.

"Fantastic!"

Nakul smiled. "I am so proud of you! I can't even think about it; Sheena would have killed me."

"You just shocked me...I thought you were serious about Sneha," Vivek said.

"Who is Sneha?" Nakul asked.

"His friend,"Vivek replied.

"My girlfriend," Jai said. He turned to Vivek. "I am serious about her, it was just a confidence thingy."

"Confidence thingy?"

"I wanted to see if I have the self-confidence to meet girls like these and face them like I did in a place like this," Jai said in a rush.

"So, what did you figure out?"

"Well, I am all red. I am clearly not cut out for places like these. I think I am a one woman man," he said and smiled shyly.

"Good for you! That's quite a realisation! It means the twenty thousand bucks are well spent,"Vivek slapped him on his red back.

Ethical Mascara

Sahitya decided to take a break from the internet business. His goodbyes were an emotional experience for the team as his participation was nothing less than extraordinary. According to the trio, he was and always would be an undeclared partner of this venture. They tried to dissuade him from going away. One evening as they were trying to stop him again, he said something which they could not counter.

"The world is a book and those who do not travel read only one page," he said quoting St Augustine.

He pinned the tag 'Happy to Wander' on his t-shirt and bid a warm farewell to his friends. They promised that they would also take up travelling. But as soon as he left, they got busy with their most important voyage – travelling through the frustrated mind of an average Indian.

The expanding website userbase did not give them much time to dwell on Sahitya's absence. He had arranged a great team so that they could continue shooting videos. The cheques, even though of low amounts, continued to add to their growing account.

They added several videos of people venting out – a Pandit of Hanuman Temple was upset that people were eating chicken on Saturdays, the assigned day to worship the illustrious God. A Delhi Transport Corporation bus driver cribbed about his long hours of driving with very little time to sleep. A librarian was angry claiming that today's youth was hardly seen reading a book in the library and this was just the beginning of the fall of civilization. And then there were students who never stopped cribbing.

A male student's video 'God is a Nymphomaniac' specifically became viral not only because of its title but also its content. A student at the Delhi School of Art stood before the camera in a pair of jeans and a kurta. He spoke with abrupt pauses to express his thoughts.

"Hi! My friends call me *thirki*. That's a funny Hindi slang for nymphomaniac. The reason they call me by that name is because I can go anywhere anytime. I can think about sex in a temple or in the classroom and not feel guilty about it. I don't even hesitate asking a woman for sex. The maximum reaction I feel I should get is a 'No'. But, that doesn't happen. Women often react as if I have threatened to rape them. And my friends seek fun in calling me thirki in the college campus. But, I want to ask you something. Doctors claim that men think about sex every seven seconds, which means that every guy in this world is a nymphomaniac. And if you observe carefully at what nature has done to human beings, I bet you would be shocked. Nature or Creator or God created this Universe and the galaxies and then the planets and gave it life. But reproduction was simple until God made human beings which became one of the few species apart from some breeds of monkeys and dolphins that have sex for pleasure. Now, why did God do that? Why were we given testosterones and estrogens? Why give us the craving for sex every seven seconds? And why inhabit us in a round planet with different time zones so that every second of every minute, someone or the other is having sex? Is this God's way to keep watching live porn? So I ask. Is God the biggest nymphomaniac ever?"

The video went viral within hours. Their total hit-count had now reached 800,000 with Sheena's still ruling at 350,000 hits. When they did a count of their revenues for the past two months, it was slightly exceeding five lakhs mostly due to brand endorsements earned by Sheena's video. They decided the time had come to pitch the website to an investor. The kind of reach they wanted for their platform could only be achieved with a huge chunk of investments from an external source. And even though the revenues were low and would not attract investors, but the fact that they were approaching a million views for their website, showed promise.

Vivek took the onus of finding the investors. He had been an investment banker and knew the right kind of people to contact for their platform. Or so he thought. Only when he started calling his previous colleagues did he realize that all those years he spent working in big corporations, hardly resulted in any friendships. One by one, they all started avoiding his calls. Vivek was embarrassed for not being able to secure even one meeting to make their pitch. But Aakash and Jai kept motivating him and he kept trying. Vivek tried more fiercely by sending presentations to even those people who were his juniors. One such colleague was Dheeraj who worked with him in the same bank. He had written a mail to him about IHAFA and he actually bothered to respond. The junior apparently had now become a portfolio analyst at a venture capital firm.

One fine evening, as they were wrapping up work, Vivek received a call from him. He informed Vivek that the Fund Managers wanted to meet them and planned a probable collaboration. They considered the call as a good omen. Vivek and Aakash started the tedious task of preparing a detailed project report for the investors and Jai single-handedly managed the show. They had five days for the preparation and Vivek's former career as a banker came in handy. Aakash's experience of failed meetings added to their proper preparation.

The night before the meeting, they sat together in their office to do a mock session of the interview before finally going to bed.

•

They arrived at the venture capital fund's office half an hour before their meeting. Dheeraj led them to a conference room. The office looked less official than they had imagined.

They felt overdressed in their formal suits. There was an atmosphere of youthful enterprise. Young employees were exuberantly exploding with ideas supported by the funding group, in an equity share arrangement.

In a few minutes, Dheeraj returned and led them to a large office cabin of one of the fund directors. As they entered the cabin, they noticed four men seated in a row behind a long desk, facing them. Oddly, there was one man sitting in the far corner facing the window. They were conscious of their attire, as they once again noticed the laid-back style. The four interviewers were in casual wear with the only exception of the man facing the window. He was a Sardarji dressed officially and busy reading a book. They were invited to take their seats. Aakash sat in the middle flanked by Vivek on the right and Jai on the left. Dheeraj took his seat north of the desk like a mediator. The interviewer in the centre started.

"Please tell us your names?"

"I am Aakash. Vivek and this is Jai," he said gesturing politely.

"Guys, we have already gone through your presentation. Dheeraj took us through it this morning. Now, we have some questions to ask."

The interviewer in the centre was quite relaxed. He didn't appear intimidating at all. The trio was confident.

"Sure," Aakash said.

"What are the current loopholes in your business?"

They shifted uncomfortably. They had also thought on these lines but they never expected the questions to start from there. Aakash glanced at Vivek as if something has been asked out of the course. Vivek decided to pitch in.

"We are quite sensitive about loopholes. We believe every business has some loopholes and there should be a constant endeavour to safeguard the business from any kind of loopholes. Currently, we suffer from loopholes in the technology and branding front, but we are sure that with the funding coming in, we can cover them."

The second guy asked a question. "How much of this business is going to be content driven and how much marketing driven?"

Aakash took the lead with an answer he had already mugged. "While this business is all about content creation, we firmly believe that it's the brand image which will keep the viewers coming in and also adding more videos to make it truly a people's platform. To answer your question, it will be a mix of both."

The Q&A continued with the various interviewers taking them through their business details, their expansion plans and of course, the exit plan for the investors. While all the interviewers participated actively in grilling the three potential partners, the Sardarji remained silent; he continued to read facing the window. The interviewers finally looked at each other. No more questions. The three felt confident at the interviewers' satisfied faces. They were almost relieved when one of the interviewers turned towards the Sardarji.

"Sattu...all yours!"

The sound of those words reverberated in their heads, making the three nervous again. This guy was saving the best for last; seemed as though this new interviewer Sattu was going to grill them badly. Sattu shut his book and placed it on the table before turning to face them. Aakash noticed that he was reading a children's comic book. He glanced at Vivek with confusion.

Sattu had an endearing personality in his own right. He appeared thoughtful, calm and composed and he spoke so softly that it sounded like he was mumbling. He gave them an introspective look and spoke in a serious tone.

"What is your take on ethical make-up?" Sattu asked.

They were confused.

"Could you please elaborate?"

"Everybody these days has an ethical identity – kind of a make-up: a little bit of soft transparency toner, an honest mascara, a lip gloss of team spirit, a moisturizer of protection, a dark kajal of responsibility... corporates, individuals...just about everybody is talking so much about it without actually doing anything. It seems that the words cosmos and ethics have come together to form the word cosmetic."

Vivek nodded. "You mean corporate social responsibility?"

Sattu shook his head. "Social responsibility gives you a forced feeling. It sounds like you have to fulfill a duty. Let's call it individual internal awareness."

"We definitely believe in..." Vivek started.

Sattu cut in. "Sorry but I want to hear each one's individual points of view."

They exchanged glances and murmured in agreement. Vivek continued.

"Sure! I think I am concerned about ethical responsibility," Sattu jumped in. "So you are not definite any more?"

Vivek tensed at the remark.

"Relax! Take your time to speak. This is not a question that you should answer in a hurry and at the same time this is not a question for which you should take a lot of time to reflect." Sattu smiled.

Vivek thought for a few moments and decided to go for the most honest opinion that came to his mind.

"I definitely believe in ethics, in morality, in transparency and I not only believe in it, I live it as a follower of spirituality, I believe in the oneness of all. I believe in equitable division of wealth so that no one remains deprived."

"Do you believe that equitable division of wealth will help remove poverty?"

"I think so," Vivek replied hesitantly, unsure where this line of questioning was headed.

"Do you think if corporations like Microsoft or Samsung turn into non-profitable organizations, it would benefit all?"

"I believe it should."

"Hmmm...interesting!" Sattu remarked.

Sattu turned his attention to Aakash. "So, what's your take on ethics?"

"I believe in ethical growth," Aakash said confidently.

Sattu smirked. "What's that? Never heard about that bird."

"It means that you become a self made man, you succeed with your own efforts, your goodwill, your network built over the years, and not take help even if you are privileged, and I can vouch for it because despite being the son of a senior IAS officer, I have never taken any kind of support from my father…that's what I call ethical growth."

"So how much did you grow without him?"

"I am trying and I will keep trying till I succeed," Aakash said with a determined expression.

Sattu smiled. "Hmmm…interesting!"

He turned to Jai. "What about you young man?You look the youngest of the lot."

"Sir, I am the youngest, no doubt, but as effective as my colleagues."

"Sattu. Call me Sattu…please enlighten me on your values."

"I believe in ethical ownership."

Sattu laughed. "Did you guys rehearse this before coming?"

All the interviewers joined in his jest while the three relaxed slightly.

Sattu glanced at the three. "I mean one guy talks about ethical equality, another talks about growth and this young gentleman talks about ownership…"

Jai nodded.

Sattu looked at him with a serious look. "Anyway, sorry to interrupt… please go ahead."

"I believe that people should completely own up to their decisions and not make others suffer because of them. One of the main reasons why I quit my job and became an entrepreneur was to have complete ownership, not only of the success but also of the failures," Jai explained with all honesty.

"Which organization did you quit?" Sattu asked.

"Best Mobile Technologies."

One of the panel interviewers piped in. "You mean because of the recent restructuring that took place?"

"Yes."

The interviewer asked again. "Were you also a part of it?"

"No sir, I retaliated and left the organization in protest. I believe that the company suffered losses due to wrong strategic decisions taken by senior management and if anybody needed to be fired, then it should have been them."

Sattu seemed to agree. "Would you agree to be fired for your inabilities even if you are the owner of the company?"

"Yes, of course!"

Sattu smiled, rubbing his hands together. "Very interesting!"

"We need some time and we shall let you know in a few days," one of the interviewers said after Sattu gestured to him that he was done.

Taking that as a hint that the interview was over, they stood up and said their thanks before they were escorted out by Dheeraj.

"When will we know?" Aakash asked as soon as they were out.

"It's a big decision. I will do my best," Dheeraj said, not giving any indication if the interview was successful.

They left feeling a little disappointed.

Yoga Se Hoga

By the time they returned from the investor's office, Vivek was tired of the repeated discussions of what the investors would decide.

Based on his experience, Vivek knew that whenever an investor said things like 'Interesting!' or 'We will get back to you!' rest assured that they would never get back. But, Aakash wanted to dig some more, make changes in the presentation and return to the investors. Jai, even though silent all this while, had something else going on in his mind. It was close to five months since they had started and he had only one month left until his parents would have exhausted the FD amount he had broken for them.

Vivek switched on the TV as soon as he hit the sofa and started watching a show called 'Bhasha Raam Bapu ka Shatak'. This was probably the best way to quieten his friend's rant. Aakash and Jai plonked down on the sofa.

Bhasha Raam Bapu was a renowned astrologer, face reader and yoga guru famous for knowing ninety-nine different languages ranging from Hindi to Urdu to Kannad to Manipuri to French to German. He had a wide variety of followers from across the globe and had created a quasi-empire by covetting government grants in the form of subsidized lands and huge donations from people. Vivek had recently started following him through a TV news channel which telecasted his daily show. The show was presented like a darbaar for common people to discuss their problems and get solutions from their Guruji. The show started with a small speech by

Bhasha Raam Bapu where he boasted that he may know 99 languages, but he is still trying to learn the 100th language of love. The crowd clapped.

After he was done, the darbaar began. A beautiful girl stood up from amongst the seated crowd on the floor and shared her problem.

"Guruji, I want to become a film star and I have been struggling in Mumbai for the past three years. On two different occasions, I was offered the leading role in films but on one condition...that I had to sleep with the producer of the film. What is your take on that?"

Guruji closed his eyes and took a deep breath. He then requested everybody sitting to move towards the right side of the hall while the girl stood in the middle. He then asked the girl to close her left eye and asked her what she could see?

"I see you and all these people sitting on the right side."

"Now close your right eye and open the left one and tell me what do you see now?"

The girl followed. "Now I only see you," she replied.

"Good...so now you know what your aim is...now let me tell you what is attraction? Close both your eyes and walk towards me."

The girl obeyed further and followed his voice as she walked towards him. She walked slowly towards the voice and finally reached his seat.

"Open your eyes now," said Guruji, his voice seemed distant now. The girl opened her eyes to find that he has now moved to the right side of the hall beyond the seated crowd.

"Do you realize what attraction is? Now let me add one more twist to your story...assume that all these people sitting here are film producers. You cannot reach me without crossing their path. Now walk towards me with your eyes closed."

The girl followed further and started making her way through the crowd, trying her best not to touch someone. But as soon as she started crossing the crowd, she started hitting people.

"Can I use my hands to locate people so that I don't hit them?"

"No, you cannot. You do not have any contacts in the industry." The girl had no option but to follow. She continued very slowly making her way through the crowd when Guruji asked her to increase her speed. She increased her speed a little and bumped into a man and fell. She got up and started moving again. Guruji pushed her further. "I need you to reach me on a count of ten. One...two...three...."

The girl was tensed, increased her speed to reach him, bumped and fell several times but ultimately made it by the count of ten. Guruji held her, hugged and caressed her.

"Now I know why this show is called 'Bhasha Raam Bapu ka shatak'." Aakash could not resist from expressing himself.

Guruji asked the crowd to take their original places and continued, "How did you feel when you reached me at the end?"

"I felt relieved."

"And how was the experience with the bumps and falling?"

"It hurt...but I wanted to reach you and you gave me a deadline."

"My deadline didn't mean that I was going to die. You could have reached me somewhere else. The moment you saw me with your left eye, your aim was clear. You kept following my voice with closed eyes and reached nowhere and finally, when you reached me you were more relieved than happy. The only time you would have enjoyed reaching towards me was if your eyes were open. Always acknowledge and embrace your surroundings and then walk towards your aim."

"So, you mean acknowledge the Film Producers?"

"Yes."

"So you think I should sleep with them?"

"Whether to sleep with them or not is entirely up to you."

"But don't you think it will be ethically wrong?"

"Ethics and superstitions keep changing with time. Choose your own."

"Son of a gun!" Aakash could not contain his excitement.

Guruji gestured to a man. He returned with a samosa and green chutney. He glanced at the girl and she accepted the snack.

"What the fuck is that?" Aakash looked at Vivek.

"That's his prasad."

"Samosa and green chutney!" expressed Jai, feeling pangs of hunger. "We will also get to eat samosas if we go to the Darbaar."

"I want to meet him but only if he meets in person, one-on-one." expressed Aakash.

"You get paid a thousand bucks if you sit in the darbaar."

"This is all paid crowd?" Jai asked surprised. "I don't mind sitting there daily for two hours and clapping for him to get a thousand bucks and free samosas."

"Let me find out his available timings," Vivek ended the discussion and walked away.

•

Impressed with and curious about Bhasha Raam Bapu, the trio had chosen an hour long package of meditation and consultation from the list on his website. There was something about a sadhu with a large following that had Aakash particularly suspicious.

When Vivek, Aakash and Jai arrived at the monumental ashram of Bhasha Raam Bapu, they were amazed with the size and beauty of the building. The visitor's lounge was luxurious with life size sculptures of various deities. The classical music added further flavor to the entire experience. They had to wait as Bhasha Raam Bapu was busy with other clients. After twenty minutes, they were led by a pretty young assistant. They followed the assistant to a small chamber and were given white robes to change into.

Once they got into the comfortable attire, they were guided to a meditative room with dim lighting and instrumental sitar resonating. They sat down on the cushions provided. Bhasha Raam Bapu finally entered the room and greeted them. He did something out of the ordinary, a little strange but they switched off their analytical side and followed. The sadhu switched on a music player and instead of gentle notes of a bhajan,

Bollywood music thumped loudly. The sadhu then did something even wilder; he danced to the lively music and encouraged them to do the same. This was so awkward but eventually they gave in to the spirit and danced. This went on for about ten minutes when suddenly he stopped the music and sat down on his cushioned podium.

"Dance is the best form of relaxation and is second only to sex," he started.

They were taken aback by his bold statement.

"You believe sex gives relaxation?" Aakash retorted.

"The best relaxation!"

"What is your take on casual sex?" Aakash asked.

The sadhu smiled and continued. "I went through your kundli. People might believe that you are a sex freak, but all you do is for the nourishment of your body."

Aakash felt nice. For the first time someone had acknowledged and appreciated Aakash's trail of casual sex. But he also warned Aakash. "Never attempt sex which makes you regret later."

Aakash recalled his lustful times at the cost of missing some important meetings. He nodded in agreement.

Guruji continued with Vivek. "Where are you lost?"

"I am trying to find myself."

"That is the purpose of all life."

"How do you try to find yourself?" Vivek asked him.

"I don't. I lose myself amongst all my followers…I feel happy."

"What do you think I should do?"

The sadhu explained, "Swami Vivekananda once said: 'Take up one idea. Make that idea your life – think of it, dream of it, live on that idea. Let the brain, muscles, nerves, every part of your body, be full of that idea, and just leave every other idea alone. This is the way to success.' If you can't find yourself, then try to lose yourself."

Vivek understood his point and felt relieved.

The sadhu turned to Jai and continued. "You know the reason I ask people to dance initially is to study their body language. Aakash tried to appear cool by doing perfect dance moves and repeating them again and again. Vivek tried to surrender through his dance something which he is not able to do in his real life. You were trying to match up initially with Aakash, then Vivek, then with me and then again going back to Aakash until you reached a point just for a few moments where you were yourself and you danced beautifully. Try and be more of yourself…you will do well."

Jai smiled, felt encouraged by the sadhu's positive thoughts towards him.

"You guys have started something important recently," declared Guruji shocking all of them.

"You guys are in a sensitive spot. I can easily slip you under any of my life improvement yagnas and make you wear rings on each of your fingers. But I won't do that. See, we are in the business of giving hope but people don't buy it till the time we don't make them feel miserable, even though we are aware that most horoscopes in this world are cyclical and circumstantial. So, what business have you all started?"

Vivek explained the concept of their venture website. The sadhu slapped his knee in amusement. "You all remind me of the time when I started my career twenty-five years ago from a small temple…look at me now. By the grace of almighty I should be the next God sitting in a temple near you."

The trio listened attentively to his ambitions.

"I think I will do a video for you." He said pondering a little.

A video from him would get them huge viewership. The three brightened immediately.

Guruji gestured and a guy entered the room with hot samosas and green chutney.

Bhasha Raam Bapu recorded a video for them the same day.

"Hello seekers! Today I will tell you a special secret. You all already know that a balanced mind comes from a balanced body and to achieve a balanced body one must practise yoga. But I have a special kind of yoga for you, secret yoga. It is yoga for the brain. It is a yoga to create the crorepati mindset. You ask me why? How can a sadhu teach this? I will tell you how. I have received direct communication from the siddhas of ancient times. They are sharing crucial knowledge that will help all those suffering in these difficult times," he said and smiled benignly.

"Have you every wondered why some people are so successful while others struggle to make a few rupees? It is all in the brain. Specific areas in some people's brain are more active. And the more activated parts lead to the crorepati brain. Now, how to activate these parts of your brain? Don't worry, I will give you all the information." There was hushed silence.

"But before I say more, many of you are wondering why I want to share this information. And being a sadhu I should preach abstinence. But I ask why? Why must you abstain? You are part of this beautiful thriving earth which is all about growth and development. As a human species, we are wired to be restless, to want more from this life and we are capable of enjoying and experiencing with all our senses. So, I say, why deny yourself what you wish to do.

"So, now you want to know what this crorepati mindset is? I will tell you about it when you come to my ashram. It is a workshop that has to be experienced, to be taught face-to-face. But for this special video, I shall give you one free sample that will prove to you that what I offer is going to make you rich and successful. Get into this simple yoga pose. Now, for the steps. Think about money. Lots of money. Now write on a piece of paper 'I Love Money' and pick up the paper between your legs. Then push your legs up in the air so that your body is resting just on your hands. Now, bend your hips and your knees forward so that the legs reach your face. What do you see? With all your energy and focus, you see the only three words that matter to you the most 'I Love Money'."

The sadhu smoothly did the pose in front of the camera and it finally seemed that earning money was much easier than doing yoga. But he continued. "Now focus on it with all your energy in your mid-brain, and visualize it there. Do this active-conscious thinking as much as possible and see how miracles happen! If you wish to know more, contact my ashram. With my blessings, you will make miracles!"

Even though the yoga pose was unachievable, the trio did realize that their platform was going to achieve new heights of viewership after this video.

•

A few days later, Vivek got a call from Dheeraj; the fund mangers wanted to meet them again. This was a positive reaction. Vivek insisted that it was the sadhu's blessings. Jai said it was the sadhu's video that did it, and Aakash said it was their own efforts. They waited impatiently in the conference room where they were served coffee. Dheeraj finally came to them. "The investors have a few more queries."

Vivek felt strange listening about the new interview round. They trudged into the same meeting room, sat in the same seats and faced the same set of interviewers, including the Sardarji sitting by the window, reading a comic book.

"Welcome back!"The interviewer was friendly.

"Just one or two more queries," the interviewer said.

Aakash nodded. "Please go ahead."

"How well do you know this Bhasha Raam Bapu?"

Vivek answered right away. "O, you mean our dear Guruji? We know him well. In fact, just last week he did a video for us on the crorepati mindset yoga. You must have seen it?"

Jai smiled. "It has crossed a million views."

The interviewers exchanged glances. The senior one responded. "Yes. In fact, to put it bluntly, because your website has already got that many e-footprints, we are willing to invest in your company. We are aware of its popularity and want to make this a professional venture. However, there are some formalities to make this official."

The matter-of-fact way this positive revelation unfolded left the three stunned for a moment.

The sardar piped up. "Are you guys here? We are planning to pour money into your business."

The three suddenly jumped up and burst out with thank yous. The interviewers smiled, nodded and said they would be in touch. They shook hands vigorously. The Sardar winked at them. They exited from the room, thanking Dheeraj along the way. Aakash couldn't believe it. "Your guruji has some magical powers man," he thumped Vivek on his back.

Dheeraj smiled. "I shall be in touch soon with all the details." They thanked him profusely, still unable to believe their good fortune.

•

Two days later, Dheeraj arranged a meeting with them, explaining details. "We plan to invest two crores in your company for a 25% stake and if all goes well, then we may pump in another four crores at the end of a year-and-a-half for another 26% stake."

Vivek laughed. "That's a decent deal."

Aakash thumped Jai on his back. "What do you think?"

"I think we should go celebrate!" Jai smiled.

Dheeraj shook their hands. "I bet you would. It values each one of you at two crores and your company at eight crores immediately."

Jai was startled with the fact that he was suddenly worth two crores. An idea and six months of hardwork could never have translated into this much money in any job of this world. He couldn't believe it. He decided to reveal his entrepreneurial decision to his parents once the funds came in.

Aakash was surprised. "But tell me something, you guys did all these calculations in such a short period of time?"

Dheeraj smiled sheepishly. "We had already decided to go for your company on the basis of our research and your presentation which Vivek sent me. And of course, Guruji's video locked it."

Aakash looked a little miffed. "I see...but even then you grilled us for more than an hour, made us wait, then called us back."

Dheeraj nodded. “Of course! To make you realize that nothing comes easy. You guys are extremely lucky.”

“And who was this sardar?” Vivek asked.

Dheeraj smiled. “Oh Sattu! He is one of the most interesting persons I have ever met. Ethical make-up is his favourite topic nowadays. By the way, he was the one who pushed for you the most.”

Aakash was incredulous. “Really?”

Dheeraj nodded. “Anyway, your contract will be ready in a week’s time. After it is signed, you will receive the funds.”

The guys were still in a state of disbelief. They were like crorepatis already, without even attempting Bhasha Raam Bapu’s yoga pose.

“You know I was worried that they would ask why we have the name ASS to our website,” Jai confessed.

Aakash looked at Jai surprised. “You were worried about that?”

Dheeraj waved a dismissive hand and gave them a little wise adage. “Don’t worry. They are seasoned investors. They don’t differentiate between ‘ass’ and ‘jazz’ till the time they get ‘cash’.”

Of the People, By the People, For the People

The contract and fund injection was sorted out within thirty days. The IHAFA upgraded their office to a better locality and was converted to a swanky facility with separate cabins for the three directors and largest shareholders of the company. This happened parallel to the hiring spree and their team of three grew to twenty with different heads appointed to handle different roles. Saket, a film maker, became the production head. Manoj came in as the marketing head while Swamy was made the technical head of the company. These heads were supported by a team of employees to handle their specific function. They even offered a position to Sheena, but she was too happy with her pseudo-celebrity status and spending time with her kids.

The fund appointed one of their directors, Mahesh, as one of the IHAFA directors to oversee the business. Mahesh was primarily a computer geek who was an early achiever and made it big at Silicon Valley. But his experience as a serial entrepreneur who had built and sold several companies made him a know-it-all man and the best candidate to manage a technology-driven business and keep track of finances and the legal aspect of the growing website.

The trio was also given positions in the company, at least on paper. Aakash was made the Managing Director, Vivek was made the

Strategy Director and Jai became the Business Director. Apart from the designations, they also received reasonably handsome salaries and Jai's worry about supporting his parents was resolved. They may have been designated with fancy titles, but still preferred to work the same way like they did earlier. Currently they focused completely on the launch of their website as a public platform.

The first few months rolled by with non-stop work. Aakash, Vivek and Jai gave their best to the company and slogged hard to prepare for the launch date. It was like a dream come true for them, to see the response increasing everyday. They were pleased to see the number of hits going up constantly. Once they opened the site to the public, they would shoot videos only for those needy cases like Tabassum or the beggar on the street. IHAFA would be open to the public to upload their videos.

Excited and nervous, the three were ready for IHAFA's launch day. It finally arrived and they invited all the fund partners to their office for a small get-together. The website was officially opened with much applause. Immediately, a parallel marketing campaign was started on all online platforms. Their entire marketing campaign was dedicated to motivate people to voice their frustrations – housewives, students, labourers, the common man, corporate executives, divorcees and so on. The online campaign spread like wildfire and people from all walks of life participated. The IHAFA promise was to maintain a window of four hours for the video to go live once uploaded on their platform.

Soon other videos started buzzing with popularity and Sheena's video finally lost its second position to another. It was a post by two corporate executives. Vinay and Vikram, working in the same department of a company, faced the camera and spoke in turn.

"Hi! My name is Vinay!"

"Hi! I'm Vikram!"

"We are here to use this wonderful platform to vent out a very genuine frustration."

"A first of its kind," Vikram said.

"But something which we are sure lots of guys will relate with,"Vinay added.

"We are a part of a huge Indian workforce that slogs in the corporate sector. People who desparately wait for Friday...people who get Monday blues on Sunday evening,"Vikram said and smiled.

Vinay piped in. "Yes! We are talking about people who feel like birds on Friday mornings – birds ready to fly into the wilderness of the weekend and why not...we all have earned it!"

"But this video is not about the 5:2 ratio imbalance of the week...it's about a bigger cause,"Vikram stated.

"It's about a factor which makes our Friday unproductive – every week, month after month, we struggle to work on Fridays. But no friends...it's not because of our anticipation of booze or sex over the weekend that makes us so, it's—"

Vinay and Vikram paused, exchanged glances. Vikram seemed embarrassed and shifted away from the video. Vinay dragged him back. "Come on man...it's for mankind."

Vikram was hesitant. "It's about this girl in office...we can't take her name," he glanced at Vinay.

Vikram was so embarrassed but managed to blurt out.

"I mean this girl...she just...she just comes to office on Fridays without wearing a bra...I mean why?"

Vinay had a supporting stance, he added, "Exactly! Why? Why the fuck can't she wear a bra? I cannot focus on work. You know the weekend before, I had to work on a Saturday because of this stupid girl. She left me no option but to stare at her cleavage, and as a result I couldn't finish a simple presentation!"

Vikram was now eager. "And that black sari and black backless blouse she wore last month. Who wears that hot stuff to office? Doesn't she realize how frustrating it can be to look at that smooth sultry back and not be able to touch it?"

Vinay seemed satisfied to end their rant. "Listen guys, we know there are a lot of guys around who are facing the fashion parade in their offices every week on Fridays. We totally empathize with all of you."

The video became widely popular overnight and drew many similar videos from the corporate circles. There were bored executives fed up of their daily routine, frustrated by office politics. Then there were the career girls fed up of bosses staring at their bodies; it led to a whole host of frustrated executives issues.

But the IHAFA was so widely accepted that it was not only the corporate executives who participated, but many others from all social and cultural backgrounds. The IHAFA online campaign 'I have a Frustrated Ass! Do you have one?' spread like wildfire across the newspapers, TV channels and online platforms.

They played effectively on the popular psyche that 'sharing solves problems' and what better platform than IHAFA where one would get to complain to the world, a willing audience. However, just as any big wave of fame and fortune brings positives, it brings with it negatives too.

A number of people criticized the business idea and blamed them for inspiring pessimism amongst the people at large. These detractors claimed that relieving frustrations on such a platform was just going to lead to more frustration outbursts, which could complicate matters. They received several hate mails as well as hate videos. Some of the hate videos also went viral adding to the platform's popularity. But the overall wave was in their favour and any form of publicity only added to the number of hits to IHAFA. The fund partners decided to encash the frustration drive and decided to inject more money, much before their promised timeline.

The IHAFA founders received invitations to various entrepreneurship forums to speak on ideation and implementation and they became instant celebrities.

On the personal front, they were trying to catch up on their lives and each other. They hardly had time to relax. Their meal times were at the workplace, and mostly consisted of pizzas and sandwiches. At times they were so exhausted that they slept in their cabin. Their bar was the car boot. The drinking though now had a short time span but had increased in intensity.

Their families reacted well to their success. Aakash who finally thought he had succeeded with the big league, sent a vintage bottle of scotch to his father as gift and in return, Aakash received an invitation to come to Lucknow for the weekend and inaugurate the bottle. Vivek finally relieved Aarti from the bondage of marriage and signed the divorce papers. Jai revealed his change of profession to his parents and presented them with a car.

The three entrepreneurs received regular remuneration in exchange for their reduced equity and passionate hardwork in growing the business. In all probability, this whole enterprise would lead to a happily ever after scenario, but, all is not perfect in an imperfect world.

Raas-Leela

The three entered into a routine. On Mondays they had a meeting with Mahesh to analyse the performance of the videos. The topmost viewed videos, the videos with most likes and dislikes, the most commented videos, the on videos with the highest rating, and new videos, were assessed at length.

One fine morning as they sat for one of their regular discussions, while analyzing latest reports and videos, they came across a video posted by a five-year-old girl for her father. Her mother, who was holding the camera, helped her daughter recite her memorized lines, and in between prompting her to continue. It resulted in a touching and heartfelt capture.

"Hello Daddy...Mommy also saying hello...Sorry, mommy says hello...and hello to all the people watching TV...." Mother whispers in the background that this is not going to come on TV. "Hello to people working on laptops...please download games for me." Mother hints at her to tell people about what you want to pray for. "Yes Mommy...I want to pray to God for three wishes – one is that my daddy gets well soon. He is very very sick, he has to drink glasses of medicine at night before dinner. And second is that God please give him more time. He says that God does not gives him time for me and mommy...and...and...and...yes don't come to my school on Janamashtami." Mommy corrects her. "Don't forget to come...please come! Ok bye daddy...bring chocolates for me."

Mahesh pointed out that this was a good sign. Their platform was being used by housewives to reach out to their busy husbands. While he continued talking, Jai's mind wandered towards Sneha. It had been months since he had actually given her any attention. He had been so engrossed in work that he had practically ignored her. Feeling decidedly guilty he felt that he had to make up for it. The Janamashtami festival reminded him of the Raas-Leela event which would be performed by kids in Sneha's school. She had fondly invited him to her first choreographed event and he had sent a usual vague answer in return. He would attend the program that evening and make up for his absence.

•

Jai drove to the function. He did arrive at the school on time, but it took him a good half hour to find a parking space. He entered the building and searched for Sneha. She was by the stage, looking gorgeous in a pink lehenga. His heart pounded and hoped desperately that he didn't end up blushing like an idiot. She hadn't noticed him yet; she was busy guiding some of the parents to their seats. He reached out to her and patted her shoulder. She turned to look and was pleasantly surprised to see him, but she hid her enthusiasm.

"So you came?" she said in greeting. The place was crowded and people walked up and down the aisle.

"Yeah...I had to...I had promised you," Jai smiled warmly.

Sneha looked at him. "Should I be impressed?"

Jai was taken aback by her sarcasm. "Not exactly, but you can be happy."

Sneha smiled widely, "See, I am happy." Her grin was so fake that he felt insulted.

She handed him a VIP badge. "You may sit in the front row."

"Hey! I didn't come here to watch the show!" The minute the words left his mouth, he regretted it.

Sneha gave him a glare. "Then why did you come at all?"

Jai quickly explained. "I just came here to see you."

"See me?"

Visitors brushed past them to their seats.

"It's been a long time since we met, no?"

"How long?" Sneha asked, her gaze narrowed. Jai was nervous.

"I don't know…fifteen days."

"Twenty-seven days!" she snapped.

"Really?" Jai asked.

"Yeah!"

Jai tried to lighten the mood. "How can girls keep a track of the exact number of days when they are otherwise so poor in maths?"

"Girls may be poor in maths but they are sensitive about the heart which beats…how many times in a minute?" she interrogated.

Jai was flustered by her attitude. "I don't know…forty-fifty times?"

"Wait!" She stopped a kid making his way to the front. "Hey Anuj… tell me how many times does the heart beat in a minute?"

"Ma'am, a normal heart beats between sixty and a hundred beats per minute."

Sneha shook her head and said, "Good boy."

Jai shrugged. "I was close."

Sneha was not looking happy. "You want to try another one?"

"No, please. I have not come here for some stupid quiz. I have come here for this stupid show." Again he regretted his words and quickly apologized, "I didn't mean that."

Sneha shook her head. "No. It's fine. If that's what you feel, so be it."

Jai tried again. "No, I am really sorry."

Sneha headed towards the back stage. "I have to go. The show is about to start. Go take your seat."

Jai was hurt. "Don't do this."

"Don't do what?"

He was in front of her. "Let's finish this first."

Sneha was fuming. "You want to finish it?"

"No...finish this argument," Jai expressed. He seemed to be getting all his words wrong.

"There is no argument...you came to watch this stupid show on my request. I am obliged."

Jai was fed up. "So, you are not going to finish this?"

Sneha was angry now. "Why? What are you going to do?"

"I don't know. I may just hug you in front of the teachers and students and their parents and the principal and peon and—"

Sneha cut him off. "Then do it!"

Jai glanced around nervously. "Don't think I won't...I may just do it."

"I am already pink with make-up, purple with anger. I might as well get red."

Jai felt his skin heat up. Sneha smiled sardonically. "Your ears are gone."

She tried to step away when he pulled her into his arms. For a moment she seemed to like it and then she suddenly pulled away. Jai was thrilled with himself.

He laughed. "Who said that a red man cannot hug a pink woman?" She blushed darker. There was a large audience and many were snickering at them. Sneha dragged him to a room at the back of the stage. It had a dressing area and lots of costumes hanging on clothes racks.

Jai looked around. "So...this is where you rehearse?"

Sneha nodded. "This is where the kids dress up."

"So where are the kids?"

"They are already on stage."

Jai smiled. "Oh! So you don't want to be around them while they perform?"

"I don't think so...they will be fine."

"You sure?"

Sneha laughed. "Pretty sure."

"You want to go watch them?" Sneha asked with a sneaky smile. Jai got the hint. "Depends on what I get to watch here."

"Oh! So you are quite hopeful," she said.

Jai nodded. They held each other close.

Sneha broke the steamy silence. "Can I ask you something?"

Jai nervously responded. "This is my first time."

Sneha shifted slightly, but didn't let go. "I know that...I just wanted to ask if—"

Jai stepped back. "Wait..."

Sneha smiled. "It's written all over your face."

Jai gazed at her with seriousness. "What if I tell you that I am not a virgin?"

"Mock me...now answer my question."

"No...first you tell me."

Sneha looked at him innocently. "What?"

Jai hesitated but asked. "Are you a virgin?"

"What if I am not? Will it make any difference?" Sneha asked.

Jai suddenly felt guilty for having asked such a question. "I am sorry. I didn't mean to."

She burst out laughing, her hands around his neck, pulling him closer. Sneha whispered. "My question was this: when you get excited, does only your face turn red or your body as well?"

Jai whispered back. "I don't know...why don't we find out?"

"So how do you want to start?" she asked.

Jai caressed her cheek. "I don't know...you are the choreographer." Outside, on the stage, the musical performance commenced with a bang. This was the sign for them to do the deed. They started with an intense kiss and she turned her back towards him, indicating to him to undo her blouse. As he removed her dupatta, he noticed she was wearing a backless blouse. He undid the strings with trembling fingers. He kissed her back and gently removed her top.

As the kids performed the beautiful and harmonious Raas-Leela, the two lovers consummated their relationship. They were spent but satisfied. Still in each others' arms, they heard the applause.

Jai spoke first. "So…what's the heartbeat per minute during sex?"

Sneha caressed his bare chest. "Anywhere between sixty to hundred."

"Oh! So that boy pretty much summed up our entire scene in an answer."

"Yes."

"How long was the performance?"

"Ten minutes," Sneha replied.

"But I can still hear them," he said.

Sneha glanced at him. "Oh theirs? It's a good thirty minutes."

"And what about my performance? Was it a good ten minutes or a bad ten minutes?" Jai asked.

Sneha giggled. "I don't know…it was satisfactory."

"What do you mean satisfactory?"

Sneha shifted. "How can I judge? It was my first time as well."

Jai couldn't hide his smile.

Sneha noticed. "You look happier with this stupid info than you were during our love-making."

Jai hugged her close. "This is not stupid info…it's a mark of commitment."

The Common Man

Jai spent the night at Sneha's place. Knowing his friends, Jai guessed that they would be dying for more details. So the next morning when he reached the office, he quickly slipped into his cabin to avoid any kind of embarrassing queries. However, before Jai could settle down, an over-excited Aakash and a smiling Vivek entered his cabin and made themselves comfortable.

"So?" Aakash said, raising his eyebrows a few times.

"So?" Jai replied innocently.

Aakash was backslapping his friend. "You did it!"

Jai still played cool. "Did what?"

Aakash smiled. "Finally!"

Jai was calm, playing with the paper weight on his desk. "Finally what?"

Vivek didn't even try to enter the conversation. He just watched Aakash trying to break Jai's calm demeanor.

Aakash paced. "You finally belled that cat!"

Jai guffawed. "What is it between you and animals...kill the dog... bell the cat?"

Aakash stared down at him. "Tell us...you got your snake out?"

Jai threw a paper clip at him. "Let me work...I am already late."

Aakash slapped his desk. "I know but did you pollen the flower?"

Vivek decided to intervene. "Leave the guy alone, yaar. He will tell us when he is ready."

Jai shrugged. "I don't know what you are talking about."

Aakash rolled his eyes. "Even a child can tell what we are talking about. If you don't tell us, we will spread the news in the entire office that you are still a virgin."

"Mean buggers!" Jai snapped.

Vivek calmed him. "Come on yaar, we are your friends."

Jai felt cornered. "Okay! Come closer. I don't want everyone to hear. Yes, we made love last night."

Aakash shouted at the top of his voice and uncontrollably rushed out into the office declaring, "My young lion has tasted blood." Jai was so embarrassed that he asked Vivek to stop their maniacal friend. The entire office discovered the truth and congratulated a red-faced Jai. Aakash's excitement turned into a disruption when he bumped into a visitor who had just entered the office.

The visitor was old, but not weak. He was dressed in a pair of simple trousers and a white shirt. He appeared well-educated. He explained the purpose of his visit.

"I have come here to shoot a video."

Aakash was pleasantly surprised. "Sure...my colleagues here will help you with that."

Aakash gestured to two of his staff members to set up the meeting room.

"Before that, I want to talk to the three of you," he said, as if he knew them personally.

They led the visitor into the conference room and offered him a seat. He took a moment before he spoke. "I have been tracking your website since the time it started and I must say that it's a very creative idea. I also wanted to do a video, but didn't have the money, so I thought I'd come here and request for help."

Aakash spoke first. "Sure, sir. A lot of people who do not have the resources to shoot their own videos contact us and we shoot it for them. You just need to fill out a simple form."

"That form requires information about me, my name, age, sex, address, occupation, income and a declaration that I own the content, is that right?" the man asked.

Aakash nodded. "Yes of course. You already know about it."

The man shook his head sadly. "See, the reason why I wanted to meet you guys is that I want a waiver regarding that."

They became concerned at his request.

The man seemed to understand their dilemma. "Trust me...the reason for such a request is not because the content is explicit or I want to trouble you. The only reason I want a waiver on the form is because I don't want people to judge me by my name, my caste or my state. I just want to speak like a common man to a common man."

Vivek expressed his concern. "Sir, we respect your thought behind the waiver but unfortunately, we are tied by some laws and processes. The form is a requirement we cannot waive."

Jai looked worried and Aakash too had a grave expression.

"You see Vivek, I am very fond of this platform and I believe that this can bring in a people's revolution in this country. But I don't want to restrict that revolution to a particular state or to a particular caste or even occupation. A revolution has to sweep the entire country, a revolution restricted to one part of the country is like a man excercising only his hands or his legs. Now, to bring in that kind of revolution, I want to make a starting point. But that starting point must not be coloured with my biodata."

The trio stepped outside to discuss the situation.

"What do you say?" Vivek asked.

Aakash shook his head. "It's impossible. We cannot go through with this. Mahesh won't allow us the waiver."

"Before we contact Mahesh, we need to be sure whether we want this to happen," Jai pointed out.

Aakash wasn't sure. "The question here is 'Can we allow this to happen?'"

Vivek waved a nonchalant hand. "Let's leave that to the lawyers."

Jai glanced over to the conference room. "The man seems simple and truthful."

They decided to call Mahesh from the speaker phone and when he answered, they explained the situation.

Mahesh was adamant. "Guys, I understand your predicament, but we can't do it legally. It is not possible. I cannot allow this at all."

"But Mahesh, can't we just shoot the video and see what it turns out to be?" Aakash enquired.

"Well, we can, but before we take it online, the man or someone on his behalf will have to own it."

Vivek quickly responded. "What if we own it?"

Mahesh disagreed. "We cannot own it. If you as an individual want to own it, then I have no problem."

"Okay thanks, we'll get back to you on our plan," Aakash said. They returned to the man.

Vivek explained the situation.

The man gave them a wide smile. "It will be a fantastic video, I assure you," he said with confidence and drank his tea.

•

They called for Saket to arrange for the shoot immediately. An over-enthusiastic and bubbly guy who would do anything to get the camera rolling, Saket arranged for it in no time. The elderly man appeared calm, composed and confident. He wasn't the least bit conscious and appeared as though he was reaching out to the people.

"Hello everyone! This is the Common Man. I initially thought of referring to myself as the Aam Aadmi, but then realized that it may get into a different political connotation given the current situation in our country. So, I decided to go with Common Man. I am a common man just like the most of us in this country, in this world. Let's try and list some of the characteristics of the common man. One, they are common, which means that they are not uncommon, which makes them completely like each other. Two, they are human beings which means that apart from an active body, they have an active mind and neuro system. Now, these two characteristics give an impression that all the human beings living on this planet are common men. But, no! The third and most important characteristic of a common man which also defines him is that a common man is born to get exploited – it's his life purpose like some kind of prophecy of God. No matter what the caste, colour, creed or country, the common man always lives to be of some use to the Special Man – the man who governs or exploits.

"I am almost as old as this country. I have seen governments come and governments go, promises made and forgotten. And every time there is an election,you know that mockery of the democratic process which we have with several parties and candidates barking their slogans and claiming to be the saviours of common man, I realize I have no one to vote for. But, they don't leave me there; they feed me with these self-proclaimed ethical campaigns and make me realize the importance of participating in the electoral process, and in deciding the future of this country. And I do it again. I go and give my stupid but important vote. But hey! That's what I am supposed to do. I am supposed to repeat my mistakes because I told you – I am a common man. But who do I vote for? I don't feel like voting for any candidate or party. So I do it the other way round. I vote for anti-incumbency. My vote is nothing but my declaration that the previous candidate was a fool. And therefore, I give opportunity to some other fool, knowing all the time that it's me who becomes a fool in all of this.

"Sometimes I feel that I should escape from my country, to shift to some other peaceful place, or may be some developed country like those superpowers in the West. But, I feel helpless to learn that the entire planet, every inch of it is ruled by some country or the other which in turn is ruled by politicians. That it is a fact that there are common men everywhere, in every corner, in every street, using their rights of anti-incumbency. Then I think who is to be blamed for messing up the entire planet? Surely, the Gods have not done their job well. They created this amazing planet called Mother Earth and let it get raped by us. Clearly what a waste of their creation. But then who created the people – clearly the Gods. This leaves me confused. Why would someone create a beautiful masterpiece and then create monkeys and give them knives to destroy it? It makes me feel angry about Gods.

"I feel like meeting them and asking them a couple of questions. Then I go to the so-called spiritual gurus and ask them to arrange a meeting for me with the Gods. They tell me that I need to renunciate everything to attain moksha. But who the hell wants moksha? I just want to meet the buggers and see if they are capable enough of running this planet, and if not, then do we have any option of replacing them? Anti-incumbency if I may say. But I don't get to vote there. No one holds elections and no one contests. It's like this never ending dictatorship of Gods. Then I feel happy – at least I have elections down here on our planet, our country. A democratic way of choosing or at least rejecting what I don't want. Anti-incumbency suddenly seems to be a lot of power.

"Then my wife tells me that you were better off when you were a drunk. You only used to crib about the food earlier. Now, you crib about the whole world. So I go back to drinking, listening music, making love to my wife and raising children for I know that this world would always need common men to survive and move forward. At the end, I would just like to recite a poorly written common man poem.

"Kab tak hawa dega apne mann ki is ardaas ko, Jab nikal hi gaya tere haath se bhavishya to ab chhoot bhi jaane de itihaas ko."

The man finished his spiel and there was dead silence. Even the cameraman forgot to say 'cut'. The man politely moved out of the frame and left. There was nothing more to be said or done. Any further conversation would have reduced the impact of his heartfelt delivery.

They filled up the form themselves and signed it. The first ever form owned by three individuals together and they instructed their technical team to feed the video online immediately.

•

The common man video elevated IHAFA to a different level altogether. A number of people followed suit and uploaded their videos claiming to be representatives of the common man, talking about corruption, reservation, women's safety, inflation and other issues, finally acknowledging the fact that IHAFA was in fact the new voice of the nation.

Aakash, Vivek and Jai felt humbled and privileged for having given such a platform to the people and this in turn led to further financial support from the investors, without diluting any equity. The money would be focused on a singular purpose – to encourage more and more people to speak up. Their form-signing spree continued as many strangers turned up emulating the original common man speaker.

On the business front, their platform crossed more than fifty million hits and advertising revenues soared through the roof.

Am I just a Number?

?

Six months into the launch, the IHAFA team reached another peak – five hundred videos. The public platform had truly become democratic with people from different walks of life uploading their outbursts on it. The investors decided to celebrate the occasion and honour the video uploaders with the highest number of views and comments. A grand gala party was arranged at one of the leading five star hotels. Before the celebration, there was an award ceremony and the three founders – Aakash, Vivek and Jai – received trophies from the investors for an impeccable execution of an awesome idea. Some of the employees were also awarded for putting in days and nights of work to set up the new company. The people who gave the initial videos to the platform were also awarded – Sheena, Tabassum, Ramakant Chaturvedi, the Bengal beauty Parnoli and the Man on the Street.

The focus of the awards then shifted to people whose videos scored highest on the platform – awards for most viewed, most commented, highest rated, most liked, fastest viral video, and so on were distributed. Vinay and Vikram grabbed the second highest viewed award followed by the Common Man who couldn't be reached. Bhasha Raam Bapu got the third position. He sent one of his disciples to collect the award.

The interviewers who had questioned Aakash, Vivek and Jai during their first pitch declared their company to be the best investment made by their fund. While they boozed and partied with all the directors of the fund, Sattu made a silent exit after the awards distribution.

The celebrations continued till dawn with more booze, smoking, music, dance, and of course flirting.

The three successful entrepreneurs drove home in their drunken avatars. They managed to get inside their home and staggered over each other before falling asleep in their suits. It had hardly been a couple of hours when the harsh ringing of their mobiles disturbed them. After many abuses, Vivek decided to take the call. It was his phone that was ringing non-stop. He tried to focus on the caller ID and noticed Saket's name flashing on it.

"What's the problem, Saket?" Vivek slurred.

"Vivek? Listen, it is urgent. We have a situation here," Saket said.

Vivek snapped awake. Saket sounded troubled. "What happened? Is everything alright?"

"I got a call from a girl that she wants to shoot a video. I told her that she could come on Monday morning, but she told me that she is already standing in front of our office."

They had these kind of eager waste-of-time whiny complainers too whose video feeds were not worth uploading. "Yeah so tell her to get lost."

"I did! I asked her to leave but then she told me something which left me with no option but to reach office," Saket said nervously.

Vivek sensed trouble. "What did she tell you?"

"Vivek, this girl has been raped. She is completely devastated. Her clothes are torn, she is injured and has been crying profusely."

"Oh God! She should be at the hospital and should report to the police," Vivek said loudly. Aakash and Jai stirred wondering what the commotion was about.

"She insists she wants people to see her current state, and then she will go to the police."

Vivek was shaking his mates awake. "This is serious. We will be in office very soon. We will also report this to the police." Aakash and Jai were by now fully awake.

"Vivek, please don't get the police. If you arrive with the police, then she will run away or she may change her mind to do the video," Saket said.

Vivek wasn't comfortable with this idea. "Then let her decide otherwise. What difference does it make?"

Saket was insistent. "Vivek! I was trying to reach you guys since the past half an hour, but no one picked up. So, I checked with Mahesh. He has given very clear instructions that this video needs to be up immediately."

Vivek was getting another call. It was Mahesh. "Okay I'll call you back, Saket. Mahesh is trying to call me." Vivek hung up and responded to Mahesh's call.

"Where are you guys?" Mahesh asked clearly upset.

Vivek stood his ground. "We were sleeping. We came back at four!"

Mahesh didn't care. "Listen, Saket has been trying to reach you."

"I know. I was speaking with him when you called up," Vivek replied coldly.

Mahesh was impatient. "We have to get this video uploaded immediately."

Vivek was level-headed. "But, this is a police case...she is the victim of a crime. She should go to the police, not the media."

"That's the whole point, Vivek. Don't you see? She has come to us. This is a big compliment for us. It means common people believe in our platform."

Vivek was concerned. "I don't know Mahesh, this is serious."

Mahesh's voice carried a firm tone. "I know this is serious, that's why I want all of you to be at the office immediately, shoot the video, and while it gets uploaded, take this girl to a hospital and let them call the police."

Vivek again tried to reason. "Don't you think we should take her to the hospital first?"

"This is an opportunity to share a victim's pain. It won't serve any purpose," Mahesh snapped.

Vivek was silent. The man was ruthless. He didn't care about the girl; all he wanted was to make sure IHAFA made more money. Vivek felt the throbbing headache of a hangover. He didn't argue.

Mahesh seemed to sense Vivek's discomfort. "Are you still there?"

"Yes."

Mahesh tried to make the conversation light. "You guys really drink like fishes, did you enjoy last night?"

The pounding in head grew stronger. Vivek closed his eyes. "Yeah."

"Let's take the party forward and help this girl. Trust me, with this video getting online, you will be the King of Internet!"

"Sure Mahesh,"Vivek managed.

"That's my boy," Mahesh said and hung up.

Vivek reflected on the situation. Mahesh's attitude reminded him of the days when he used to work in the corporate sector. He felt the suffocating pressure. His mobile rang again. It was Saket.

"We will be there in fifteen minutes."Vivek said and hung up.

Jai and Aakash snapped into action at his words, while Vivek updated them on the latest development.

•

When they arrived at their workplace, they noticed that Saket had kept the shutters lowered.

"She's inside," he said as he opened the shutter. Still battling with their intoxicated brains, the trio headed to the conference room where the victim was waiting. Through the glass wall, they could see her disheveled state. She appeared miserable and helpless. Her dress was torn at misappropriate places and bruises were visible.

They were shocked. Jai could barely look at her. Aakash tried to keep himself together even though he was agitated to the core. He wanted to go and kill the bastard. But he did manage to keep up a straight face. It was Vivek who handled the situation sensitively. He gently gave her a glass of water and introduced himself. She accepted, took a sip and gave it back to him with trembling hands. He politely explained that he understood why she had come, and she could shoot whenever she was ready. She nodded.

Saket had already set up the recording room, ready for the shoot anytime. She got up and Vivek led the way. As she moved, blood stains were visible on her trembling legs. Vivek offered his support but she refused. It was disturbing to watch her stagger in her crumpled bloody state. They entered the room. She stood at the marked position and faced the camera.

Vivek gestured to the cameraman and he repositioned the camera to make one singular shot to show her full form. He offered his jacket to cover herself, but she refused that too.

Unable to take in the scene, Jai finally shuffled away. But his friends dragged him back inside.

The rape victim faced the camera. The cameraman indicated to her to start. She fought tears and emotions to speak in a wavering but determined voice.

Am I Just A Number?

"My name is Neha. I am a History student. Last night, I was picked up by some goons from outside a gurudwara. They dragged me into a van, blindfolded me and drove me to a deserted house. When the blindfold was removed, I found myself in front of Rajendra Yadav, the local MLA who was active in our college elections. He had tried to flirt with me during the elections, but I had avoided him. I never realized that history would repeat itself, that these politicians are nothing less than kings and have full authority to pick any girl from the road and take her to their harem.

"Rajendra Yadav was the first one to pierce my soul after which he threw me to his followers...like people throw bones to their dogs. They scratched and ravaged me completely. For them I was just a number – Rajendra Yadav's 57th, somebody's 22nd, somebody else's 17th. And I don't remember how many of them violated me as I fell unconscious. When I woke up, I found myself near the banks of Yamuna river watching pundits worship the rising sun. I could have gone to the media...the police...I badly need a doctor...but I decided to come here. This is a people's platform. So, I ask everybody who is watching this video. Am I just a number?"

Tears finally rolled down her eyes as she turned silent. Vivek signalled the cameraman to stop shooting. Saket picked up a declaration form and showed it to Vivek, but he told him to wait. They guided her out of the recording room and requested that she should go to the hospital with them. Before she could respond, there was a knock on the shutter. Vivek asked Saket to check who it was. A young guy in his twenties was standing. She told them that he was her brother, so they let him in. He had parked his car outside and wanted to take her to the hospital. The girl looked totally drained and wasn't able to stand. They quickly bade them goodbye and assured them the video would be uploaded that day. They headed to Jai's cabin to update Mahesh.

"Is it done?"

"Yes, it's done," Vivek replied. "We will upload now."

"Good...how is she? What's her name?"

Vivek checked the form. "Her name is Neha. She was gang-raped by some local MLA and his goons."

"Oh God! That's terrible...where is she now? You should take her to the hospital."

"Her brother came to get her."

They disconnected the call and continued to ponder over the situation. Something was bothering Saket.

"What's wrong?" Jai asked.

"She has not signed the declaration form."

Vivek nodded. "That's okay. We will sign it...we have signed it multiple times."

Saket was still nervous. "It's a rape case."

Vivek thought about it and nodded. "We couldn't have asked her or her brother to sign it."

Saket was worried. "Do you want to talk to Mahesh about it?"

Vivek felt the urge for coffee to kill his pounding headache. "No, I don't want to talk to Mahesh about it. He is the one who initiated this in the first place."

Aakash was silent throughout, suffering the pangs of a hangover. "I agree with him. She was in a bad state. In any case, we could not have asked her to sign the form."

Saket shrugged. "Okay, if you think its fine..." They all nodded groggily.

Saket brought in the form and the three of them signed it and uploaded the video soon after. Saket gave them a concerned look and headed out to get the coffees. Even though he didn't say anything but they could gather from his face that their signing the forms could have legal repercussions. Law suits and hate mails were not new for them. Ever since they had taken this platform to the public, they had received hate mails from someone or the other and some had been severe enough to be a part of team discussions. But even after discussions and appropriate reverts, haters never seemed to calm down. Some of the more aggrieved parties also filed suits against the company. But the trio and their investors including their aggressive director Mahesh had carefully hired one of the best law firms to take care of it.

Kahani Mein Twist

The impact of the video was colossal. It created a huge uproar amongst the people and the three found themselves locked in their office the entire day, trying to avoid the media. Most news channels picked up the buzz on the video and ran it throughout the day as if there was no other news to cover. The media questioned them about the girl – her full name, her address, her whereabouts – but they didn't know, so they said they wouldn't divulge such information. They were clearly not equipped to handle the media and answered their questions at an emotional level.

The police claimed that there were no reports filed. The media and police searched for the girl in various hospitals, but she was nowhere to be found. The media declared the day to be one of national shame. They speculated that the girl's disappearance might be because she committed suicide or was too ashamed to come out in the open. Social media was overwhelmed with the video shares and there were many strong comments about the nasty face of Indian politicians.

Nonetheless, the accused, MLA Rajendra Yadav was not spared by the media. An army of reporters from various channels and newspapers were stationed outside his house. The opposition demanded that he be made to resign from the government and sent to jail immediately. Rajendra's already tainted image was completely ruined in public, even though he claimed that he was innocent.

The search for the girl continued throughout Sunday and Monday, but there was no trace of her. On Monday evening, Aakash, Vivek and

Jai went home early. They needed to unwind. They were stressed out completely and decided on neat scotch.

Aakash contemplated as he sipped. "But why didn't she go to a hospital?"

Vivek gulped his down, and poured a double. "And she looked like she needed a doctor badly."

Jai offered a different viewpoint. "You never know...her brother might have decided otherwise...you know family shame, respect and such."

Aakash swallowed his drink. "What fucking respect?"

Jai challenged him. "You don't know about the lower strata of society, Aakash. They are very concerned about their social image."

Aakash wasn't accepting that. "But she herself decided to speak up."

Jai nodded. "That was her decision. But once her family found out, maybe they didn't want her to come out in the open."

Aakash was on this third peg. "How can people be so stupid?"

Vivek agreed. "Did you talk to the SHO?"

"Yes. He says there are more than eighty Nehas studying History in Delhi, but none of them matches her description," Aakash said.

Jai voiced his irritation. "I don't know why this is happening to us, and look at the media reporters."

"They are like sharks, hunting for some meat," Vivek responded.

"My parents are wondering what's going on, they've been hounding me with questions," Jai said uneasily.

Vivek shared that concern too. "Mahesh told me that there was a lot of pressure on them from the MLA's party. They want to do an investigation in our office."

Aakash gave him a questioning look. "What kind of investigation?"

Vivek shook his head. "You know how these politicians are. They want to make sure they don't get implicated or blamed."

"Did you talk to your Dad?" Jai asked Aakash.

"Why should I talk to him?"

Jai shrugged. "He was trying to reach you."

"I don't need his help."

Vivek saw his expression.

"Don't you think he might just be concerned about you?"

Aakash shook his head. "He knows I am in trouble. He just wants to show off his power, his contacts in the government to get me out of this mess."

Vivek and Jai looked at each other.

"Trust me...I avoid him because I respect him."

Jai piped in. "You respect him? So you avoid him?" Jai asked.

"Yeah...No! Don't confuse me. I don't respect him because I avoid him. I avoid him because I respect him."

Jai didn't want to know. "I give up on your stupid logic! I give up on the rape victim. And I give up on this messed up world."

They tried to get some sleep but ended up having a restless night.

•

It was just seven in the morning when Vivek ran into his friends' rooms shouting and waking them up with much excitement. He was ranting about the NEWS reported and created such a ruckus that Aakash and Jai woke wishing that Vivek do his regular meditation routine than run around like a chicken without a head.

"What's going on?" Aakash asked sleepily.

"Is this your new yoga exercise?" Jai yawned and stretched.

Vivek gave them a rough shake. "Guys can't you hear me! She's been found! She's on the NEWS."

Aakash and Jai, shocked and fully awake, joined him. They watched the newsreporter explain that they had been able to locate the girl in Meerut. The Delhi police ensured the girl was admitted to a government hospital. The channel boasted of their investigative journalists who located the missing girl before the police could find her. They blamed the police for supporting the ruling party so that MLA Rajendra Yadav could escape the DNA test. The opposition bombarded the government and demanded an immediate DNA test. Given the public involvement in the case, the ruling party had no option but to send Rajendra Yadav for the test. They switched off the channel feeling relieved with the latest development.

Aakash muttered. "Will they be able to prove that she was raped by him? I mean it's been more than three days now."

"Let's see," Vivek wanted to leave the matter to rest.

Jai scratched his crotch. "Let's hope they do. I am fed up of the journalists."

Vivek's phone rang and he answered. "It's Mahesh," he told the two, and they returned to their cosy beds.

"We just watched it on TV," he said to Mahesh.

Mahesh sounded relieved too. "Time to relax. I know the last couple of days were tough on all of us, but the bugger is now under the scanner. With the DNA test coming out, you never know…the government might topple. One video on our platform and look at the impact. I told you buddy, you will be the king of Internet."

Vivek didn't like his style, but he had to admit that the power of their platform had brought judgement to a politician.

Mahesh told them to take the day off. Vivek shared the news with his sleeping friends. They were already in a 'day off' mood.

The next day, they returned to work as usual. They settled down to their routine and called up Mahesh to conduct their postponed Monday morning meeting. They discussed the recent turn of events, evaluating the videos and analyzing the impact of the current video on the future of their platform. Just then, they noticed a piece of shocking news on the TV hanging on the wall in Mahesh's cabin.

"Am I just a number? Yes, you are!"

The news channel announced the update of the rape kit test and the DNA test conducted. The doctors declared that the victim was not raped, there was no indication of forced sex, and the victim had had consensual sexual intercourse. The most surprising twist was that it had happened after the date of rape claimed by her. They also declared that the semen found did not match with Rajendra Yadav, but with the man she claimed to be her brother. The police had taken the girl into custody.

Aakash was the first to react. "What the fuck?" he said as they all stared at the screen.

Mahesh was in hyper mode. He was afraid of the impact and got down to controlling the fallout. He asked them to get together and have everything clear in their heads. He instructed them to re-enact the series of events that Saturday and moved out to talk to senior fund managers.

Aakash, Vivek and Jai could not figure out even for an instant that she was lying – her attire, the wounds on her body and face, her constant sobbing, her body language and the way she faced the camera – everything had seemed so real. Mahesh entered with the area SHO. The SHO was accompanied by four constables and they took up the cabin space. Mahesh's tense expression made it clear that they were in serious trouble.

SHO looked at them sternly. "Vivek Sharma, Jai Chaddha, Aakash Srivastava...*tum teeno ho?*"

They nodded to confirm.

"Tumhari complaint hui hai. Warrant nikla hai. Thane chalna padega tum logon ko," the SHO said.

Aakash stared at him with anger. *"Kya baat kar rahe hain aap?"*

"Neeche chalo aur sarkaari jeep mein baith jayo," SHO said firmly.

Aakash didn't back down. *"Aap mazaak mat kijiye hamare saath,* please."

SHO looked angry. *"Mazaak to tum logon ne kiya hai. Aur kaun kaun bhai hai us laundiya ka?"*

They stared in shock for his language and tone.

Mahesh quickly intervened. "Guys, I think you should go with them. Don't worry, I will talk to our lawyers and get this sorted out immediately."

Aakash was controlling his temper. "You better! We are innocent of any crime."

Mahesh nodded furiously. "I assure you. I will be there at the police station very soon with our lawyers."

The three voluntarily agreed to go with the police. The staff gaped at them with shock as the SHO gave orders to the constables to seal the office. All the staff members were told to leave and the office was locked down. The three friends sat in the police jeep and were taken to the police station. At the station, they constantly called Mahesh but either his phone was busy or he didn't pick up. Later, they found that it had been switched off.

SHO led them to his office and instructed them to sit across from him. *"Kya bawandar macha rakha hai tum laundon ne? Kya naam hai tumhaari website ka?"*

Jai said softly. "www.ihafa.in"

SHO looked at him, "Phul phorm?"

Jai spoke hesitantly. "I have a frustrated ass dot in."

SHO smirked. *"Batao, aisa naam bhala rakhta hai koi apni buzzness ka? Arre buzzness pooja ki tarah hota hai, usse lachchmi aati hai, tumne usmein apni gaand ghusa di."*

A peon arrived with glasses of water and placed them on the table. SHO gestured. *"Lo paani piyo! Waise bhi ab kuch nahin ho sakta, saade chhe baj chuke hain. Aaj raat to tumhaari ander hi kategi."*

They stared at him in dismay.

Vivek looked at him. "Sir...*kya hum ek phone kar sakte hain?"*

SHO smiled coldly. *"Do karo."*

Vivek called up Mahesh again, but his mobile was switched off. Odd. He tried the number of one of the senior directors at the fund, but no luck. Aakash felt helpless and reluctantly decided to call his Dad. He called twice, but there was no answer. He left his dad a message. The SHO noticed their futile attempts.

SHO seemed to enjoy their predicament. *"Ho gaye phone? Layo, apne-apne phone yahan jama kardo."*

Vivek tried to appease him. "Sir, *aap please samjhiye. Hum log padhe-likhe log hain."*

SHO leaned back. *"Sir aap bhi pleaze samajhiye, main bhi BA pass hun. Anpadh sirf vo hai jiske kahne pe ye arrest hua hai."*

Rajendra Yadav's reference pushed Aakash to give his Dad's reference.

Aakash gave him a sharp look. *"Aap samjhiye sir. Links hamare paas bhi hain."*

SHO sighed, looked at the clock. *"Kyun time kharaab kar rahe ho?"*

Aakash added, *"Mere Papa Lucknow mein IAS hain."*

SHO grimaced, then shouted. *"Tere Papa Lucknow mein IAS hain to kya poore des pe dhauns jamayenge?"* He gestured angrily to submit their phones.

They kept silent, switched off their mobiles and handed them over to the SHO. One last glance at the station entrance for any sign of Mahesh or the lawyers, there was no one. The three were exhausted from the day's events. They were led to a cell, pushed inside and locked up by one of the constables. It turned out to be the longest night of their lives. The filthy cell was foul and had cockroaches.

The initial few hours were torturous. In soft tones, they discussed their life, recalling incidents in chronologically; from the award nights to the time the SHO bombarded their office. They were haunted by the memories of the girl they had helped. It didn't seem like a con. They kept glancing outside, hopeful that someone would come any minute and get them out of the hell hole. Aakash somehow had this undying hope that his father would bail them out, an odd attitude, since he never wanted any favours from his father.

After a few hours, they sat on their haunches and leaned against the wall. Their confidence was heavily dented. This was not supposed to happen to them. They were intelligent entrepreneurs with a good background and great education, and despite all that they were conned. It affected them deeply. Vivek tried to practice meditation. 'Let each thought come and go. Just watch them without getting affected.' But he too failed miserably. Each thought which came and went affected him deeper than the previous one.

When the tin plate containing their unrecognizable meal clattered on the floor, they avoided even looking at it. They had no appetite and no intention of eating something that looked like mush. But the sadistic hawaldar who had brought their food warned them with the dark shade of hopelessness that their stay might last longer than that one night.

Just after midnight, as they reflected on the past, trying to kill time and waiting for the next morning to arrive, they heard strong, confident footsteps approaching their cell. The intensity of the footsteps increased in urgency. And in seconds, they saw a silhouette in front of their cell. The harsh light of a bare bulb illuminated the face of their unexpected visitor – Rajendra Yadav.

The hawaldar placed a chair for him and he sat on it with one leg resting on the other. Dressed in a white safari suit, eyes red with the effects of booze, he smoked an imported cigarette and appeared spent, but relaxed.

The trio were surprised at his presence; they stood up and approached the bars, nervous yet curious as to the purpose of this monster's visit in the dead of the night. He smiled as he flicked the ash from his half burnt cigarette.

"You wonder why I have come to see you, eh?" he spoke in his broken English exuding charm, probably never having had such educated opponents.

"Tell me! Why did you do this to me? Why? I am a good person. Good MLA. I have reduced water bills. I remove garbage. I promise women safety. Why did you try to destroy me?"

Aakash felt the need to clear the air. "Sir, we had no idea that the girl..." but Yadav cut him sharply, "*Chup...Behanchod!*" Aakash was shocked at his brazen style. They realized that Yadav was not there to discuss; he was there to assert his authority, to threaten.

Yadav continued with his charade. "When the girl speak, the whole country listen. Now it's my turn. When I speak, you listen." He threw the cigarette butt, with a gesture to the hawaldar standing by to light another one for him. The hawaldar like an obedient servant, obliged.

"Your father called," Yadav told Aakash. "When you meet him tell him he is only a bureaucrat. We people run the government. We run the country." He took a pause, then continued.

"You guys are young...yuva shakti but look at yourself...look where you end up, behanchod...behind bars...because you are rotten with bloody western culture...bloody internet and social media...internet is the biggest curse...any dog barks on the internet...and you call it business? What business? Your business is dead. It's over. That kutiya didn't get gang-raped. She gang-raped you. She fucked you!" he declared laughing loudly and his chamchas standing behind laughed with him.

He stood up suddenly and approached them. He spoke in the language he was comfortable in. *"Kuch aur kar lo...internet pe...sabun becho...shirt becho...pen-pencil becho,"* he said realizing that he was speaking in the wrong language and asked one of this guys to bring some whiskey. A glass of scotch reached him immediately and he gulped down a large portion in one go, regaining his lost confidence and returning to the foreign language. "Sell anything on the internet. In the America, you can also sell yourself," he winked and laughed heartily. His chamchas were monkeys, mimicking his laughter.

Vivek decided to intervene in a polite tone. "Sir, we are really sorry for what has happened...please trust us."

"Trust?" Yadav cut again. "You trusted her?" he asked them but they kept silent. "You trusted her?" he asked again loudly and they nodded in return. "And then what happened?" he gulped the remaining peg.

"You are the finance man?" he asked. Vivek nodded. "I also have a finance institute – Maa Vasihno Devi International Institute of Management. Very foreign – all Russians and Israelis," he commented.

He gestured to a guy and he arrived with some fast food – pizzas and burgers. He placed them in their cell. "I know you don't eat jail food, so eat this. But from tomorrow, you get used to jail food." He moved as close as the bars would allow. He looked them straight in their eyes and simply said, "There is no escape."

He guffawed and his chamchas chorused his laughter as they all walked away. The three friends exchanged glances, horrified of what just happened. The night was going to be long.

•

The next morning they waited with desperate eagerness for the jail clock hanging on the opposite wall to strike nine.

"The courts must have opened by now," Vivek said, feeling hopeful of the new day. Aakash kept pondering over the fact that his father could not get them out of jail. Was Yadav right when he said that his father was just a bureaucrat or was it that he did not have enough time to act the previous evening? Maybe he would try again and make sure that they were out of prison. Jai was suffering a different kind of tension altogether. He kept thinking about how his parents would react when they discovered that he had spent the night in jail.

They waited, pacing restlessly, gazing at the clock which inched from nine in the morning to one. With no communication from anybody from the outside world, they began to worry as Yadav's last words echoed in their minds.

"Do we actually live in anarchy? Is democracy a sham?" Aakash thought without sounding his views to his already nervous partners.

The same hawaldar arrived with the food and a smirk. He noticed that the fast food Yadav gave them last night was on the floor, untouched. They had even declined breakfast. So the hawaldar gestured if he should take away the lunch as well. Aakash gestured to him to take everything away.

But before the hawaldar could leave he gave them some information, probably because he felt that he should give something back to them. He crouched low and whispered. The three moved closer. The hawaldar told them the shocking news.

"Vo ladki randi thi GB road se. Usko kisi Pratap Singh ne paise diye the ye karne ke liye. Abhi aur investigation chal rahi hai. Waise to usne Opposition *se kisi ka naam nahi liya lekin kaam to unhi ka hai. Ab koi chota mota gunda Pratap Singh, Yadav Saab jaise aadmi se kyun panga lega?"*

They stared in disbelief and exchanged shocked glances. Before they could ask more, the hawaldar slipped away. Was he another one of the liars they were fending off lately? They thought about it long and hard. The hawaldar was probably right. It was a political conspiracy but the three of them, stuck in a jail cell, were on the wrong side of it, suffering the brunt.

For the next few hours, the three friends sat in a circle contemplating the possible scenarios. Countless thoughts, both positive and negative, crossed their minds as they discussed everybody, right from Mahesh to their investors to Yadav and finally Aakash's father. They even discussed the legalities around their bail and were excited to recall some of the minutest details from their memories of various experiences they had heard and read in the news. Brains can really work when stretched. Right from the timings of the court, to some laws on imprisonment to the rights of the Indian citizens, they discussed every perspective they could think of, often looking at the clock which seemed to be moving rather fast.

The clock moved well past five in the evening when the courts closed. Still no sign of anyone to get them out. As the clock touched eight, they lost all faith and it became abundantly clear that this was going to be their second consecutive night in jail. What they could not fathom were the events which would have occured outside with no one bothering about them. Nobody had turned up to meet them during the day. Would Yadav turn up again tonight or was that a special appearance? They lay down on the ground, their minds and bodies getting used to the filth and stink. Aakash was the most restless and could not believe that with all the contacts his father had, he could not get bail for them. The hawaldar arrived with the food again, this time looking concerned. He placed the food on the floor and made, a comment which made them think about consuming it. *"Khaana chahe kitna bhi ganda ho, ander jaake taqat hi dega."* They looked at each other in agreement. Skipping food one more time would have been difficult for them. They managed to swallow the overcooked rotis and soupy daal.

They had nothing more to discuss than to wait for the next day with anticipation that something might happen.

The next day, their minds were more blank than anticipatory. Their hearts were heavy and frustrated. They waited for some angel to turn up but not with the same sense of enthusiasm. Just when the day was over and darkness spread its dreariness in all directions, they heard their names being called from a distance. Somebody was discussing something about them. They tried but could not recognize the voice. It definitely did not belong to Mahesh.

The Price of Freedom

After fifteen long minutes, the hawaldar came up to them and opened their cell gate. *"Tumhari bail hui hai,"* he said. It was the best four words they had heard in a long time. They rushed out of the cell and reached the SHO's table. They noticed Sattu sipping tea. He gave them a big grin and they were surprised that it was him who bought their freedom. It didn't matter. They were so relieved that someone from the fund had come to save them and gestured their respect to Sattu.

SHO grinned mocking them. "Beta, everyone knows about it now, you have become phamous."

They were shocked that they were now a news item. They exited the SHO's cabin to the common room and saw their faces flashing on TV. The channel showed their photographs and reported their arrest two nights ago. The channel further claimed that the entire episode was a planned sabotage to topple the government and to particularly damage the image of MLA Rajendra Yadav. The IHAFA founders may have had a hand in planning the sabotage. Rajendra Yadav was seen making a small speech.

"Bhaiyon aur behnon...Is duniya ne Sita maiya tak to nahi baksha aur unhe tak agnee-pareeksha deni padhi thi...to main to aap logono ka ek chota sa sevak hun...mujhe ek chota sa DNA test dena padha to kya hua? Aap logon ki seva mein main hazaron aisi pareekshaon se guzar sakta hun...magar humne bhi kasam khaayi hai...ek sachche Hanuman bhakt ki tarah na hi Sita maiya ko dhund nikalenge balki Raavan ki is Lanka ko bhi jala ke aayenge."

After his short but intense speech, the reporter announced that the weblink to www.ihafa.in was now inactive and the website shut down. The fund which owned 51% of the company had also decided to pull out as they felt the website was being misused.

The three were flabbergasted. This was the strangest turn of events. Sattu suggested that they go to the fund office immediately. They hired a cab and switched on their mobile phones to find a flurry of calls received from their families.

Aakash noticed several missed calls from his Dad and called him to inform that they are out now. But, instead of asking more about his well being, his Dad cribbed more about the fact that he could not manage a bail from a petty MLA. Vivek calmed his parents and assured them that everything was fine. Jai's position was the worst. He spent half the time trying to get his mother to stop crying and the other half trying to compose Sneha.

They arrived at the fund office and without wasting any time, they barged into the fund director's cabin. He was surprised to see them, but behaved politely and offerd them a seat. "So good to see you. How come you guys are out?"

"Mr Sattu got our bail...aren't you aware?" Aakash asked.

FD smiled. "Oh I see! That's good, typical Sattu. I am surprised because our lawyers just left the office five minutes ago to get you bailed out."

The FD looked at them with a serious expression. "I completely understand how difficult it must have been for all of you. We were shocked to see this happen, and the media just blew it out of proportion. I mean look at the news channels, they are all filled with negative stories about you and the platform."

Aakash eyed him suspiciously. "We saw the news too. Is it true that the fund has decided to pull out its investment from the platform?"

FD squirmed. "We will talk about it, Aakash. But first tell me, did you guys eat anything since morning?"

"We haven't eaten anything but I want to discuss this first," Aakash said with a hard look.

FD looked at them. "Why don't you guys freshen up, eat something and then let's discuss how to take things forward."

They moved to the conference room and ate sandwiches silently, but wondering what's going on in the fund director's mind. Once through, they returned to the director's cabin. They entered to find three more directors and Mahesh as well in the cabin. They were welcomed and offered sympathy for the turn of events, especially the last two nights. The three took their seats and waited to hear the other side of the story.

FD started. "Before I say anything on our behalf, I want to admit that in my thirty-five years in the financial sector, I have never faced this kind of situation. No matter how much we tell you that we understand your pain, I don't think any one of us can actually understand what you guys went through. But, there are definitely certain lessons for all of us. The first and foremost is that processes and procedures are laid out for a reason and should be followed to the dot. The second lesson is to not take decisions hastily – Mahesh and you guys just rushed through to get this video online."

Vivek was blunt. "We did not. It was Mahesh who was eager to make us the 'King of the Internet'."

FD looked irritatedly at Mahesh, who looked guilty. FD turned to the trio. "Please let me finish. The third and most important lesson – never handle the media without consulting your bosses."

Aakash stared at him. "Sorry? I thought we were partners."

FD shook his head. "Don't get me wrong son, but you would agree that our experience is far greater than yours. We could have handled the media much more strategically. Anyway, the fact is that we love this platform. It is our fastest growing business today and would probably give us fantastic multifold returns on our investments. But, the bitter truth of today is that we have decided to shut it down. We had no other option."

"But, why can't we continue?" Jai asked.

FD looked surprised. "How can you even ask that? The three of you signed the declaration form of that girl yourselves."

The three glared at Mahesh. "He is the culprit, why is he standing silently?" Aakash snapped.

Mahesh was about to say something when the FD stopped him with a hand gesture.

Vivek looked at him with a disbelieving expression. "Is it just about the form? Do you mean that you would have continued our website if we had not signed the form?"

FD smiled. "I know what you mean, Vivek. Things have become much more complicated than just signing on a dotted line. Unfortunately, we are stuck right in the middle of a political rivalry."

Aakash retorted. "There are other ways to resolve this. We can go and meet Rajendra Yadav and tell him that we had no idea behind this unfortunate incident."

FD and the other directors all shook their heads. "Don't you think we already tried that? We literally begged him to take the case back. But he was very upset and very adamant. His image was completely tarnished and he blames us for that."

"And you think that Yadav has an impeccably clean reputation like Seeta?" Jai smiled coldly. "Now our image is tainted sir, the media has ruined us, due to no fault of ours!"

"You should know who has the power in this town. This is the reality, no matter how unfair. We have sorted it out with that man and he promised to give us a clean chit, including the three of you. In fact, our lawyers have updated him that the website is no more functional. You guys are young. You can come up with so many ideas," the FD finished in an appeasing tone.

Aakash was simmering with anger. "And what's the assurance that those ideas will not get ruined by the likes of Rajendra Yadav?"

FD was not happy about his behaviour. "Look Aakash, every idea is not so politically vulnerable. Come up with something else, something with a little bit of constraint, within our boundaries."

Vivek broke into the conversation. "Sir, is there any way that we can continue with this business."

FD nodded. "There is one way in which you can take charge of the business, even though it is highly advisable not to do so."

Vivek, Aakash and Jai looked eager.

FD smiled. "You get an investor and take over this business from us. Buy us out."

The directors nodded in agreement. They had made their stand quite clear to them: we won't do this business and we won't let you do it as well. The three exited the office with deflated spirits and wandered the streets aimlessly. Their wounds were fresh and the pain of failure and regret immense. How could life completely rupture in a matter of few days! They kept walking silently, lost in their own thoughts when they suddenly noticed a huge poster of Bhasha Raam Bapu at a chouraha. They decided to meet him.

•

They arrived at Bhasha Raam Bapu's house. It was late in the evening, probably not the best time to show up, but the guys who had been robbed of everything and had spent the previous two nights in prison could hardly think about these pleasantaries. The guard checked with Bhasha Raam Bapu and showed them the way to the drawing room.

After they waited for half an hour, Bhasha Raam Bapu showed up with the same serene smile which he had pasted on his face and probably was on display even while he slept. They greeted him. He behaved as if he was expecting them. A sevadar arrived with glasses of warm milk. Bhasha Raam Bapu explained the entire turn of events as they drank the milk.

"Times have changed, but not for the first time. Times always change. But in this dynamic world, they are changing faster. And we as mature youth of this country need to change faster than the times," he started off, setting the tone of the conversation.

Bhasha Raam Bapu went on to explain the damage their platform had caused not only to the likes of Yadav, but to the general public. "This kind of platform can only complicate things," he explained and wanted them to understand that life is full of opportunities. They nodded in agreement. Debating over his arguments seemed redundant. The sadhu had become the voice of Yadav.

"He is a simple guy. He just wants to serve people. He is even of the same clan as Shree Krishna and follows Karma blindly," he said. The sadhu seemed to be Yadav's biggest brand ambassador. Despite the fact that they wanted to leave his house immediately, they let him finish. He was instrumental in expanding their platform, but as he rightly pointed out: "Times had changed."

After they had listened to him, they went to their office and found a shutter on the gate. Their office which just a few days ago resonated with vibrant energy had suddenly become a dead spot of bad memories. They wandered aimlessly, lost in their whirlwind thoughts and arrived home after three hours. They went to their separate rooms and crashed.

Happy Gods

The trio slept the entire next day, completely isolated from the outside world and woke up after sunset. In the meantime, Rajendra Yadav's press release announced that the fund and the founders of IHAFA were relieved of all charges. He claimed that the founders had met him and apologized to him for the fact that they started this stupid platform. The three friends received emails from unknown people requesting that IHAFA be relaunched. Saket and several other employees called up to share their concern and were sympathetic.

When they were through with their calls and sat down for their evening drinks, their phones beeped messages simultaneously. Each had received a message from Sattu – 'Hey Confused Bastard...come to my place tomorrow evening at seven' followed by his address. They wondered what he meant by calling each one a 'Confused Bastard'. Their curiosity was piqued and they decided to meet him. In any case, a message from one of the investors was looked upon as a ray of hope.

The next day, before they went to Sattu's place, Jai decided to see Sneha. That afternoon, he popped over to her place. She lived in a small flat just a walking distance away from the school where she used to teach. She didn't waste time asking him irrelevant questions about how things were and how he was. Instead, she hugged him – a nice warm bear hug. Jai melted in her arms, his eyes wet. He needed that hug so badly. A genuine human touch was soothing to a tormented mind.

They didn't stop there. Their hugs became more intimate, kissing and feeling each other. But, right at the moment when two lovers surrender themselves, Jai stopped. Something held him back. Sneha understood and didn't comment. Instead, she pecked him on his forehead, smoothed his hair and gently disengaged. She ordered lunch. The food arrived and they chatted about new movies, restaurants, bars and their hangouts. But their physical proximity, Sneha's light touches and her warmth got Jai into the mood. He told her about Sattu's invitation. Sneha encouraged him to go.

•

That evening the three guys arrived at Sattu's home on time. Sattu was in the garden, tending to his plants with much affection. As soon as he saw them, he waved a hello and gestured them to go to his drawing room. Sattu excused himself and went to freshen up.

Contrary to their perception, Sattu's home seemed quite modest for an affluent man. They wandered around the drawing room and noticed strange wall hangings and knick-knacks displayed on various tabletops. They noticed images and statues of Gods. These were not paintings from renowned artists or artifacts purchased from auctions. These images were not even meant for worship; they appeared more artistic than mystical depicting Gods in a very novel way. The Gods were in a cheerful avatar – chatting and hugging each other, shaking hands, dancing and generally appearing to have a nice time.

The trio was totally engrossed in these portraits and paintings. Like overawed children, they gazed and studied the intricacies of each portrait. They could not contain their laughter at the sight of all deities chatting up sitting inside a chamber and on the blockaded gate were the words 'NO ENTRY', while outside a mob of people tried to push one of the spiritual gurus through the gate.

Aakash, Jai and Vivek did not even realize that Sattu had returned to the room. They finally noticed him smiling. They settled down on the cushiony sofas, while they still gazed at the wall hangings.

Vivek was enthusiastic. "This is amazing! I haven't seen anything like this before. This is such a happy union of Gods – so positive. Where did you buy these?"

Sattu smiled with satisfaction. "I conceptualized them and had them commissioned through my artist friends. You won't find this kind of stuff in the art market."

Vivek was surprised. "But how did you get the idea? And why?"

"I was not happy with the way artists depicted Gods. Whenever I gazed at the images, I felt sad. Then I wondered why Gods never laugh or have fun? I realized the problem is not with them, but with our portrayal of them, we have probably taken them too seriously. So, I got these done assuming that if the Gods are happy, then I will also be happy and vice-versa. I call them 'Happy Gods'."

"That's fascinating…I never really thought of it from that perspective," Vivek exclaimed.

"So, you guys are a bit relaxed now?"

Aakash was serious. "Not exactly, but far better off than being in jail. Thank you so much for bailing us out."

Sattu waved a nonchalant hand, gesturing it was nothing.

Aakash nodded. "We still don't know how to handle the damage done by the media. We seem to be the villains in this whole unfortunate incident. In fact, yesterday we got an offer from Meera Juneja's secretary that she wants us in her show. We can at least do some damage control by appearing in her show."

Sattu laughed. "I think you guys should just sit tight right now. Any more publicity would only make the situation worse. And don't worry about your defamation. People have short term memories. Besides your prison news was covered by channels for just two days, and I doubt many people would have registered it properly."

Vivek was satisfied to hear that an experienced guy like Sattu felt like that.

There was an awkward silence. They were waiting for Sattu to reveal the true purpose for inviting them over.

Sattu read their minds. "You must be wondering why I called you here. Well, to make a long story short, I want to help you."

His words sounded magical to them and they leaned in, their undivided attention on the man offering a lifeline to their sinking lives.

Sattu warned them. "But my help would be of a different kind. My help will make your foundations strong so that events like these do not shatter you."

"What kind of help would that be?" Aakash asked suspiciously.

"It's really quite simple. I will mentor you, guide you, and hopefully you would have clarity about what you really want to do."

"Clarity?" Aakash snapped.

Sattu smiled. "Yes! Aakash, you have always been the overimaginative one. Don't worry. I am not going to drug or hypnotise you. We will just chat like friends about certain aspects of life and enrich each other."

Jai asked tentatively. "So, what are we chatting about?"

Sattu smiled. "Jai the open-minded, genius kid!"

The servant brought in a tray of food and drinks. Sattu helped himself to a plate of snacks and encouraged them to do the same.

He continued. "I will be discussing basic things like your background, your choices, your aspirations, your influences, etc."

They were all famished. Aakash was eager to query further. He chewed and swallowed quickly. "Sir, that's all fine. But we thought you have called us to help us get our platform running."

Sattu made his drink. He sipped his whiskey soda and smiled with satisfaction. "My dear fellows, even though you may decide that you do not want to go with what I have to offer you, and it's absolutely free of cost by the way, I understand. But as far as the website is concerned, I was not the only investor. It was a collective funding. I can try and influence the other investors but only to an extent. I can try and mediate for the amount at which you can get the website back, but only after you find someone else to back you."

Aakash wanted clarification. "So you are saying that you can try and reduce the amount at which we can procure the website?"

"Yes, I can try, but I don't know if it will happen."

Jai piped in. 'Sir, can't we get the website live again on our own?"

Sattu shook his head. "My partners will not allow it. And even if the website is running, the political brass will make things difficult."

Vivek tried another tack. "What if we go through this module? Would you still help us with the negotiations?"

Sattu made himself another drink. "If you go through this module, you will be so self-sufficient, that you wouldn't require my help...you would be able to negotiate by yourselves."

The awkward silence crept in again, doubts were clouding their minds. What kind of wizardly charm did Sattu possess that he could change their fates?

"What exactly will we be doing?" Jai asked.

"It is straightforward life chats. Our minds are crowded with everday stress, and we leave a lot of unresolved issues in our hearts. Unless we consciously address each and every past issue that affects us, we cannot move forward. It's called conscious awareness, facing the feelings – good and bad."

"You are a spiritual master?" Vivek asked.

Sattu laughed heartily. "No my friends, no. I am no master, no slave!"

"Why us?" Aakash asked, still suspicious.

"Because the three of you are a perfect team. You will do great things in the future, and I don't like seeing such potential fall apart and die. Your talents, your drive, and your inspiration come together and create a powerful force. And that is what I want to bring to the forefront. Currently, you are all consumed by self-pity, and are behaving like whiny selfish men!"

They gaped at him.

Sattu merely smiled. "Think about it over the weekend and come back on Monday morning, and let's have breakfast together. I am not Lord Krishna to take you through Geeta Saar. We will chat like adults and enrich each other. Until then, enjoy your weekend, get drunk, get laid and have fun."

His last words changed their perception of his module. Whatever he was offering suddenly seemed so cool. They had their snacks and drinks and left Sattu's hospitality with a positive sense. They arrived home and discussed whether or not to take up Sattu's offer.

"So, we basically have two options: either we go through his transformational module or we hire him as our mediator," Vivek said, cutting Sattu's suggestion to a two-point checklist.

Aakash quickly responded. "I think we should go for the second one. Even though I kind of like the guy, but a fucking module?! What are we talking about? We are not some sick freaks or kids who don't know what they should be doing? We created this platform and persuaded the investors to put a huge fucking amount of money in such a short span of time!"

"I agree. Even though I always wanted to talk about myself and my life with some experienced senior person, I would give preference to the platform," Jai said mildly.

Vivek looked from one to the other. "Do you guys really think that he will help us as a mediator in getting us a good deal when he himself is one of the investors? I mean the price reduction will be his loss as well."

"We've been conned and dumped with the blame, and fucked twice over. I have trouble trusting him." Aakash was totally against the idea of Sattu. "We will be polite, but at least we won't waste time with him. He will probably call us for a couple of meetings and we will figure out what he is really after."

Vivek was thoughtful. "Let's assume that we manage to get the platform back...are we really ready to run it?"

Aakash snapped. "Why not? We all have had the experience, and we're seasoned, plus we already have a fan-base. Look at the emails. People want the platform back."

"Agreed. But even then I feel that we should have an open mind regarding Sattu. Remember, he was the one who pushed forward the funding of our site," Vivek said logically.

Aakash mocked him. "You are still not over with your fetish for the gurus, right? You think he is some Bhasha Raam Bapu who will make us dance on some Bollywood numbers and give us a couple of business tips? Give me a break! This is not Mahabharat and he is not Lord Krishna. There are no Pandavs or Kauravs here. This is a globalized world. We are the Pandavs and we are the Kauravs. We want Lord Krishna and we also want the fucking website!"

While they were in the middle of the discussion, Vivek's phone buzzed. It was a call from the secretary of Meera Juneja, one of the leading TV journalists of the country. She again insisted that Meera wanted them on her prime time show 'Straight from the Heart'. Vivek told her that he would get back to her. When Vivek mentioned the call to his friends, Aakash jumped and said that they should definitely go for the show; it would help to change people's perception of them. But Vivek felt otherwise.

Jai stayed out of their opposing views, which seemed to be like a fight between a monk and a lion. They were back to Sattu again.

"You need to think logically, not emotionally, Aakash," Vivek said in a calm tone. "Let's talk to Sattu about both options. The whole idea of accepting his module offer is to try and understand him. He said good things about us, complimented our partnership. He sees something special in our combined abilities. I suggest we meet him on Monday and we tell him that Sir, this is Kalyug and we are the modern hybrids of Pandavs and Kauravs and if you really want to help us, please keep that in mind."

Jai smiled. "Sounds good to me!"

"Okay okay fine!" Aakash muttered furiously. "The son of a bitch has got us by the balls."

Confused Bastards

?

On monday morning, they arrived at Sattu's home promptly and were seated in the dining room. On the way they passed the drawing room and could not help but look in. The dining room had a different theme altogether. The long table had images of devils suffering from overindulgence. There were these ogres suffering from obesity, constipation, acidity and all other tortured poses, quite graphically depicted. Sattu entered the dining room and greeted them. He took his seat and ordered breakfast to be served.

"You have a different theme for every room?" Jai asked in awe.

"Not every room. My good wife does not allow me to explore the bedrooms. She liked the drawing room and allowed me to keep it and she tolerates the dining table design. I had to convince her that these images would discourage my over-eating habits and help me reduce weight. I have one more room in the house at my disposal – that's my reading room."

Sattu leaned back, satisfied. He sipped his chai. "So, what have you guys decided?"

Aakash and Jai looked at Vivek to take the lead in the conversation. Vivek nodded. "Sir, we feel really honored that you invited us to your home and offered us your hospitality and your mentorship. We definitely want to go for it as we have always wanted someone to guide us."

Aakash gave him a hard stare for this sudden change. Vivek was supposed to discuss the two options, not jump in and take a decision. The devil must have got to him. Aakash was tempted to blurt. Vivek gave him a warning glance that he hadn't finished speaking.

"It's just that we would really appreciate if you could help us get our website back as well,"Vivek added.

Sattu nodded. "Fair enough. Let's do one thing. Let's go through the module and if at the end of it, you still feel that you need me as a mediator, I will do it."

"Good idea!" Aakash said.

This whole module thing sounded dubious. "So, how long is the module?"

"It depends, it can get over in a week if you are flexible enough..."

"Then shall we get started?" Aakash asked.

Sattu led them to his reading room. All the walls and ceiling were painted in the color of the rising/setting sun. A wall rack of books, floor to ceiling, was the highlight of the two-wall space. They sat on the floor cushions placed in a circular fashion in the middle of the room. The room had a mystical freshness which was enhanced by the whiff of old books. Subtle undertones of instrumental music added to the peaceful atmosphere and they were already in a calm state of mind.

Sattu announced the obvious. "Welcome to my den! A place for rejuvenation, reading and reflection."

Vivek glanced at the high shelves. "So you have read all of these books?"

"Not all. I keep adding to my collection. I don't think I will ever be able to finish all of them. Some of them I open to relish the smell and texture of the pages. I make sure that I touch all of them. Let us begin."

They all nodded in agreement.

"Like I said, we will just open up to each other and chat like friends so the first step is to open up. Aakash...tell us everything about yourself."

Aakash hadn't expected to be the first target. "Everything?" Aakash suddenly looked uncomfortable.

"Don't feel embarrassed, you are amongst friends. You can just take us through the main events of your life."

Aakash agreed, he noticed his friends looking eager. He started off slowly, but gathered confidence and spoke easily.

"So as you all know, my name is Aakash Srivastava. I was born in Delhi to an IAS father and a socialite mother. My upbringing was in a lot of cities including Chandigarh, Amritsar, Surat, Ahmedabad, Hyderabad, etc. My father has always been quite active in his career and managed to get postings in places undergoing development. I have literally heard and seen discussions on globalization in my house – how India is going to develop, which places and sectors are going to do well. I have witnessed the telecom revolution with my dad signing the approval for the initial towers in front of me at our home. In fact, now that I think about it, my journey coincides with India's journey so well. I too explored my youth appreciating different women, as India explored its developmental phase. We both made some mistakes but moved on. The exploration never stopped; even now, I feel like an explorer."

Sattu nodded in approval. "That was quite thoughtful. So, where is your father now?"

"He is posted at Lucknow."

"And your mother is with him?"

Aakash looked down. "No, she expired a long time back."

"So, when did you start living away, Aakash?"

"Not sure, when I was around twenty-one and shifted to Delhi for my MBA."

"How often do you visit him?"

Aakash shrugged. "We talk over the phone at times."

"When was the last time you met him?"

"A couple of years back."

"So you went to Lucknow?"

"Actually he was in Delhi for a conference. He invited me over."

Sattu looked at him with a straight face. "Do you miss your mother?"

Aakash looked up agitated. "What kind of a question is that?"

Vivek and Jai were surprised at this line of queries. They had never seen Aakash so vulnerable. He was always tough and strong. But Sattu maintained a straight face. Aakash took a moment to respond.

"Yeah...I guess...I mean we didn't have the best of relationship. But she still gave me her time. At least she never lectured me like my dad who left no opportunity to make me realize what a waste of a human life I was. At times she used to take me to her parties. I learnt a lot about communication from her. She was such a natural."

"Okay, when did you realize that you wanted to have your own business?"

"My Dad always wanted me to be an IAS officer – you know be the key controller of the country's developments. But I realized that the businessmen, specially the industrialists, contributed as much in the development of the country. So I thought, why not be a private player? And play along as the nation progresses."

"Why ihafa?"

Aakash responded easily. "Truly democratic...it strengthened people," he glanced at Sattu. "So, are you through with me?"

Sattu gave him a knowing look and smiled. Even though Aakash had finished talking about himself, the major events of his life had triggered some emotions which he had avoided to face and didn't expect to revisit.

Sattu nodded. "For the time being. Who's next?"

Vivek raised his hand eagerly, while Aakash looked at him with interest.

'Well, I was born in Firozpur. I had a normal childhood with both my parents focused on one and only one thing – my studies. My father had a small furniture business and did decently well for himself. My mother had always been a housewife. I surpassed all their expectations topping in school, cracking the prestigious IIT entrance exam, then topping at IIT, then cracking the IIM entrance and finally topping there as well. I got one of the highest pay packages from the campus and got into Investment Banking. I worked my way up very soon and participated in a couple of big deals and visited various beautiful countries. My life was a dream ride until I got married to Aarti."

Vivek looked sad and turned away as if he couldn't face his past.

"That's when I failed miserably. Always excelling in my professional life, I turned out to be a loser as far as one relationship was concerned. My idea of marriage was more acaedemic than real. I gave all the material comforts of life to Aarti, but could not give her intimacy. In return, I expected her to behave like an ideal wife, which probably she was in her own right. But I never agreed that I was a bad husband. I started visiting astrologers, trying to put the blame on my messed up planets. And then a time came when I went into this adventurous journey trying to find my way through spiritualists, religious gurus, psychiatrists and even went to a past life regression therapist. Sometimes I took her along. I wanted her to realize that it was not me at fault, not realizing that I needed to take responsibility for my actions."

He finished his introduction with a long sigh.

Sattu nodded. "Seems like there is a lot of learning there."

Vivek was taken aback at his frank confession. "I guess so. I don't know how I managed to say so much about myself."

"That's probably the aura of this place. Where is Aarti now?"

"We got divorced."

"So Vivek, why become part of www.ihafa.in? I know you didn't do it because of the idea!"

"Well, I wanted to escape from my monotonous life, and didn't want to go back to the corporate sector which reeks of superficiality."

"Thank you, Vivek, that was quite enlightening. Now, let's hear it from the cute Punjabi boy," Sattu said.

Jai started slowly.

"I was born and brought up in Saharanpur. My father has a sweet shop there and my mother, like most of the women there is, a housewife. But she occasionally helps my father during the peak season. I have an elder sister who is married. I had a mixed childhood. I was pampered by my parents and at the same time they were strict about my studies. But even with their discipline, I was always an average student. I could never ever attain distinction. I was so average that my father had to send me to a private college for an MBA. But, I enjoyed my childhood. I relished it. I grew up spending a lot of time with my cousins. But that's also the time when I noticed the hypocrisy in my own family. All my uncles and aunts would come over for holidays, but would not party together. All the uncles would gather in one room and booze while the aunts would be in the kitchen and would supply them with snacks. So, when some one of that generation's elders blames this generation for drinking and partying, at least they should realize that we don't segregate."

Sattu smiled. "Do you have a sweet tooth?"

Aakash giggled. "This guy cannot finish a meal without sweets!"

Sattu returned to Jai. "Why www.ihafa.in?"

"I always wanted to do something of my own, and then lately, the atmoshphere at my office went from bad to worse, so I thought it was time to take the plunge."

Sattu stood up from his couch and walked around silently. He slid his fingers across some of the books on his shelf. He then turned towards them and gathered his thoughts before he spoke. "You know, one of the reasons why I collected all kinds of books and why I like to meet more and more people is because whenever I read a good book or whenever I meet people, I realize how people are the same everywhere. These two activities have strengthened my belief in the phrase that 'Man is a social animal'. And I have arrived at a theory which I call the Confusion Theory. People, all kinds of people – rich, poor, ugly, smart, fat, slim – have this urge of proving themselves to the society at large and to do so, they make choices, often choosing things they would not have chosen otherwise. It's like a syndrome, a contagious disease which spreads not only by touching, but by breathing, thinking, speaking, listening, in fact any kind of human activity. But at the end, it leaves you confused."

Vivek glanced at him. "So you mean to say that we are easily influenced by each other all the time?"

Sattu stopped. "Right! To give you an example, do you remember the American wave which swept this nation in the late nineties? Everybody wanted to move to America and settle down there?"

"Yeah...my parents pushed me a lot,"Vivek agreed.

Aakash added. "My dad gave me an ultimatum, he said either you become an IAS officer and live a royal life in this country or you move to a place like America."

Sattu grinned. "Exactly! That wave was nothing but social influences. Today, as we talk, we witness a new wave in this country – of entrepreneurs."

Aakash glanced at his friends. "Is there anything wrong about that?"

"It's not wrong for the nation. But it becomes a matter of right or wrong when you just follow it mindlessly."

He gazed at each of them. "I have come to the conclusion that you all are nothing but 'Confused Bastards'."

He watched their expressions change. One was furious, the other looked irritated, and the third merely gaped.

Sattu smiled. "Why are you looking at me like that? Think about it. Aren't you guys confused? You all did something which you really did not want to do."

Vivek was still irritated. "We may to some extent agree on the 'confused' bit but why 'bastards'?"

"Have you ever seen a confused person getting support from anyone? Does anybody out there, leave aside your investors, think about your family, but will anyone out there support you if you are not clear about what you want? Ergo Bastards!"

Aakash simmered. "So it's not really an abuse? Its non-support!"

Vivek still didn't like it. "So, who are the Confused Bastards?"

"The whole world is full of them...we all are Confused Bastards!"

Aakash challenged his point. "But there are people who have absolute clarity about what they want?"

"I assure you that their absolute clarity came only after they had gone through their confusions. Think about a housewife, doesn't she get confused about which vegetable to make for dinner? Or an executive, doesn't he get confused which shirt to wear to office?"

Aakash appeared surprised. "But these are very basic things, how does it affect clarity?"

"Decision-making and confusion is a basic trait of all human beings."

Vivek was interested. "But why is it bad?"

Sattu smiled. "In fact it's good, confusion means that you are still alive, that your brain is working, that you have options to choose from. Confusion helps you explore, it makes you sharp, you go through your choices and evaluate them."

"Then what's wrong with it?" Jai asked.

"It's not the confusion that's the problem, the problem is with indecision. You get so confused that you are not able to decide and then finally just go with the flow, with what society expects. That's what's wrong."

Jai seemed to understand. "How does anyone sort that out?"

Sattu smiled proudly. "Welcome to the module! That's what it is all about. And the first step in sorting out your confusions is to accept the truth."

"Okay, so we should just accept that we are confused?" Aakash asked.

"Not just like that…the acceptance process should be fun and memorable."

"What do you propose?" Vivek asked.

"I propose that you face the camera, give a brief intro about yourself and admit that you are a Confused Bastard."

"But why before a camera?" Aakash queried.

Sattu looked at them that it was obvious. "That's what you philosophied with www.ihafa.in. You need to face the camera and speak up, it's more dramatic and straight forward. It was your ideology."

Aakash had no answer to counter that. Jai was open to the idea. "So when should we do it? Can we do it at home?"

Sattu shook his head. "It's not homework…it's a classroom assignment. You have to do it here."

Vivek smiled as if he was joking. "You mean right here, right now?"

"Absolutely!"

He exuded a childlike enthusiasm and disappeared behind one of the book racks and returned with a camera and a camera stand. "The latest one in the town…7D camera for amazing clarity and sound effects."

They were surprised at his swiftness.

Vivek spoke up. "Oh! That was very quick. You really want us to do it right now?"

Sattu continued to set up his equipment. "Why not? Let's record it now."

Aakash added his own concerns. "Don't you think we should come back tomorrow after some preparation?"

"Come on, Aakash…there is no need to panic," Sattu said placing the camera on the tripod. "So who is the first one to come forward?"

They exchanged glances. Sattu realized that no one was going to volunteer.

"Jai?" Sattu called.

"Sir, me?" His voice was a squeak.

"Call me Sattu. We are friends now, come on. We will start with you."

Jai got up reluctantly and headed slowly towards the wall against which Sattu had set the seat.

"Don't worry. You will do very well…I have full confidence in you."

Jai waited nervously for his instructions. "Start off with your brief background and then admit that you are a Confused Bastard."

Jai gave his friends a determined look, then faced the camera and started with Sattu's instruction "Start!"

"Hi! My name is Jai Chaddha and I am an entrepreneur. I was born and brought up in Saharanpur, completed my MBA, worked with the corporate sector for several years and then forayed on my own. I admit that I am a Confused Bastard."

Sattu cleared his throat. "That was a nice try, but we will roll again. This time I want you to open up!"

Jai nodded okay.

"Just speak about your confusions – what is it that confuses you about life?" Sattu said, focusing the camera and hits record.

Jai took a few moments to think. He inhaled a deep breath and started.

"Hi! My name is Jai Chaddha. I was born and brought up in Saharanpur. I have always been under the influence of someone or the other. Initially, my father influenced me and I felt that I should take care of my family sweet shop. But by the time I finished my education, I got influenced by the numerous job opportunities offered by MNCs and the attractions of city life. As a result, I came to Delhi. Then there was a time when I was confused whether I was really happy working for a corporate. Every time I visited my home, I felt happy with the still life of a small city, the simplicity and warmth of people. I was confused whether I should really go back to my hometown and join my family business. I didn't. The big city life had damaged me completely and I now enjoyed the complexities more than the simplicities. Then I got influenced by people starting off on their own – the new age businessmen known as entrepreneurs. And now I stand here in front of you trying to understand what I really want. In a nutshell, I admit that I am a Confused Bastard."

Sattu was hopping on one foot and the other. "Fantastic! That was an Oscar winning performance, Jai!"

"Thank you!" He felt surprisingly relieved, having admitted his confusions. He sat back down and Sattu gestured to Vivek to come forward.

Vivek stood facing the camera. "Hi! My name is Vivek Sharma and I lived a major part of my life what others can describe as the quintessential middle class dream life. I topped through my acaedemics and was a hot shot Investment Banker until the day I got married and realized that life is not a classroom. My unsuccessful marriage…and by the way it was unsuccessful because of me…made me think about a lot of things. What is life and why am I here? Who is God? What is it between a man and a woman that their relationship can be so charming and yet so disturbing? I chased after astrologers, gurus, psychiatrists and increased my confusion. I don't know whether this exercise with Sattu is going to be useful, but I want to admit two things: First, I never thought that I would open up so much in front of somebody in our second exclusive meeting, and secondly, I am a Confused Bastard."

Sattu nodded excitedly.

"I hope we are not going to put this on social media."

"Not at all. This is for our own purpose."

Jai noticed Aakash was tensed, which was strange because he was always out to show that he was better than them at everything.

"Come on Aakash…let's hear it from you."

"I don't know Sattu…I am not feeling up to it."

"I leave it up to you, Aakash, you can perk it up, say whatever and in whichever way you want."

"I mean, confessions about confusions and spilling our guts to say that we are Confused Bastards should be recorded cinematically."

Sattu mocked, "So what do you want? Should we do it in the open, spread some leaves, add some background music to it?"

Aakash smiled. "Yeah, why not? I believe it's a life changing exercise."

"Okay…give me a few minutes. I will be right back," Sattu said rubbing his hands together and hurried out.

"What are you up to?" Vivek asked Aakash in irritation.

"I don't want to do this whole bastard thing…I agree that man is a social animal, that there are influences and all that crap but I am not going behind the camera to admit that I am a Confused Bastard!" Aakash said.

Jai was upset. "Why did you let us do it?"

Aakash shrugged. "Your life, your choice."

"But it felt good to spill my guts in front of the camera. It was quite a liberating experience."

Aakash got up and paced. "What the fuck is he up to? Why is he asking us to do it in front of the camera? Trust me, there is something fishy."

Vivek was defensive. "Do you really think he is going to do that? You yourself opened up with him. He is trying to help us out. Come on man, don't be such a dukkar."

Aakash glared. "What did you say? Dukkar?"

Vivek glared hard, "Yes! It's not an abuse. It's sarcasm. Whenever I find someone dragging in life, I call him a dukkar."

"But what does it mean?"

"Back in the eighties, my father had a Fiat Dukkar which used to drag more and run less."

Jai looked at his friend. "Please just do it, Aakash...do it for our friendship."

"Fuck you and your friendship!"

"Fuck you back!" Jai snapped.

Aakash was surprised by Jai's reaction and was about to give it back when Sattu entered with a servant and instructed him to take the camera to the terrace.

Sattu turned to Aakash. "Well, I have arranged for a dramatic ambience."

Aakash muttered under his breath but he couldn't back out. They followed Sattu to his terrace which was covered by a green glass shed. One of his servants was ready with rotten leaves whereas another held a table fan. Sattu had some old torn curtains hanging as a backdrop. The sunlight fell throught the glass creating the light appropriate for the camera.

Aakash was left with no option but to oblige. He made a heroic entry facing the camera. He had the perfect expression, as if he was going to reveal his ultimate truth. He paused on the mark on the floor.

Sattu gave the instructions before he snapped: "Action!"

The table fan was switched on. The curtains lifted and the leaves swirled. Aakash began with confidence.

"Hi! My name is Aakash Srivastava, son of an IAS officer. I was born in Delhi, brought up in several cities of India. Schooled in science, my graduation was in humanities and my MBA in Marketing. I started my first business soon after, when I partnered with some friends and launched a website. It didn't succeed so I switched to the restaurant business in South Delhi, which again didn't click. I didn't lose hope and soon after that, ventured into my third business in engineering education. Ha! And what a useless effort! I forgot that there are more engineers than donkeys in this country. Then I explored a website business by the name www.ihafa.in which did well, but didn't last."

He took a deep breath.

"For all you aspiring men and women, this shows that the main reason for not succeeding is that I didn't persist long enough in any one business. As a result, I lost interest and the whole self-made man ideology went to pot. I think the same logic holds true when it comes to girls. I start dating a girl and immediately lose interest. But, in this fast-paced instant meal world, what else can you expect! I openly admit to being a Confused Bastard."

"That was bloody pathetic! You cannot just say it so casually," snapped Sattu. "Say it with passion so that the whole world understands what a CB you are."

"I think the whole world will be able to figure it out!"

"You better listen to me! You wanted this entire set up, the flying leaves, and all this crap simply to spill your gut and I provided all of that. Now, you have to tell the truth my style – with energy!

Jai and Vivek exchanged glances. It was a battle of wills and egos. Not that their glances remained serious for long. But this time they were concerned. As if reading Sattu's mind and what his 'style' entailed, Aakash's face turned red and his jaw worked with repressed anger. He retreated to his position and started his oration.

"My name is Aakash Srivastava. Look at me. Look at me, all you mother fucking people living on this crazy planet. I have never stuck to one business or girl in my entire miserable life. But I was not like that. As a child, I used to be extremely focussed. But two major events made me the way I am today – puberty and globalization. And both those fucking events gave me endless possibilities in business and sex. And today, facing this fucking camera is a guy who does not know what to do with his life and whom to fuck. In a nutshell, I am a Confused Bastard!"

They all clapped thunderously. Sattu's face was filled with pride as if he had achieved his life's purpose.

"Brilliant!"

•

They returned home, but their minds still dwelt on their camera recordings. Aakash checked the weblink for IHAFA and felt disappointed to see the inactive status. But Jai and Vivek continued to exchange grins at Aakash's expense. Life had taken an unexpected turn. They settled down to the usual – booze and music, but it was a day for some soulful ghazals.

Jai and Vivek continued to mutter and giggle at Aakash. Aakash sat down heavily. "Enough guys…let it go."

Their snickering converted to laughter.

"What is so funny about it?"

"You know, there were only two things funny in your video – puberty and globalization," Jai laughed.

"Don't be stupid. Did you notice how aggressive Sattu got as I spoke?" Aakash asked, changing the direction of the talk.

Vivek shook his head. "You troubled him – you wanted all this extra stuff."

Aakash paced restlessly. "This was our first day of this module and we already admitted that we are bastards. Trust me! In tomorrow's session, he is going to give us our new fathers…"

Aakash was interrupted by his ringing phone. It was Sathiya.

"Hey Sahitya, how are things? Where are you?"

Vivek and Jai perked up when they heard Sahitya's name.

"Hey Aakash! I am in the South African jungles making a documentary about how tigers mate."

Aakash laughed. "Ask me if you need any tips."

"I was skimming through the Indian news online. Crazy stories! Are they all true? What happened?"

Aakash explained the entire situation to Sahitya, including the current one where they admitted to being Confused Bastards.

Aakash asked him about his views on the way forward. Sahitya felt that Sattu's conversations seemed to be a good starting point for the way forward. He advised that it might also help them think about better ideas to get their website back. Sahitya laughed, "Don't let the politicians screw you again!"

He hung up promising that he would be in touch and would also think about IHAFA.

Aakash seemed to be a bit more relaxed after the call but the friends didn't talk much. They continued their drinks in silence. The day had triggered several thoughts in their minds and they wondered what was in store in Sattu's unusual method to dig deep into their psyche.

•

Jai met Sneha the next day before going to Sattu's place. Sneha was sensitive and concerned about him. Jai updated her on everything. When he told her about Sattu, he realized that he spoke more enthusiastically. With a childish exuberance, he conveyed how he had opened up and how he felt relieved for admitting that he was a Confused Bastard. Sneha broke into an uncontrollable laughter.

"I was worried about you Jai, but this Sattu has given you a smile on your face," Sneha, said and hugged him. "I'm sure everything is going to be great." His enthusiasm and his appetite were getting back to normal. More than anything else, he was optimistic about the situation turning around in the future. Sneha was convinced that Jai would get his business back. They spent several hours at the coffee shop holding hands and chatting.

Hey Ganesha...Wass Up?

They were back in the mystical reading room – Sattu's Den.

"So, how did you feel after spilling your guts on camera yesterday?" Sattu asked, rubbing his hands in glee.

Vivek explained succinctly. "I felt relieved, like a child who feels good just because someone has heard him out patiently."

"That's true. That was also one of the qualities of www.ihafa.in. People felt a sense of relief because they were being heard."

"What makes it meaningful is the anticipation that by releasing the problems verbally, the situations will improve," Jai reflected.

"That's very intelligent of you Jai. It's always the anticipation of positivity that brings excitement to life. The anticipation of romance that lovers feel before meeting is more romantic than romance itself," Sattu explained.

Aakash had earlier decided to stay quiet but felt the urge to add his opinion. "The anticipation game is a deadly game. I played it with the SHO who arrested us."

They all looked at him with anticipation.

"What did you do?" Vivek asked.

"Nothing much. I just looked at him with anger when we were moving out. A meaningful look that I am going to come back for this, that I am never going to forget the horrible night I had to spend in that place."

Sattu mocked. "I am sure the SHO must be thinking about you. So let's take the module forward. The toughest part is over. From now on, everything will be easy-peasy. You just need to make friends."

Vivek looked dubious. "Make friends?"

"Yup…just go ahead and make friends," Sattu said vaguely.

"With whom?" Aakash asked.

Sattu waved an expansive hand. "With everybody! Make friends with Gods, with fellow human beings, with animals, with plants."

The three exchanged glances wondering if Sattu had gone mad. "Make friends with Gods? Seriously?" Aakash smirked.

"Yeah, seriously," Sattu said.

Aakash looked at him cynically. "This sounds fun…please enlighten us how?"

"Go talk to them."

Aakash was agitated. "Talk to whom?"

"The Gods!" Sattu responded in a relaxed stance.

"How?" Aakash asked incredulously. "Should we just kill ourselves and reach their chambers?"

Sattu laughed. "You don't need to kill yourselves. Just go look at them and talk to them."

Aakash shook his head. "That is tomfoolery, total madness."

Sattu looked surprised. "You mean to say you have never spoken to them before?"

"Obviously not…I mean who does that?"

Sattu looked at him as if he was mad. "Everybody does that! You did that at least when you were a child. Didn't you request God to give you good grades or even before that to make the exam easier for you?"

Aakash recalled his childhood days when he used to pray at times, initially before exams but later the praying was replaced for good performance during his sexual encounters.

"So you've talked to God?" Sattu exclaimed.

"That's not talking, that's praying, talking is when the other person responds."

Sattu laughed. "Just because the other side does not speak in the way we do does not mean that the other side is not responding. The other side always responds because the other side is also you."

His comment led to silence as they tried to grasp the deep wisdom in his words.

Vivek tried to understand. "Do you talk to God?"

"Ofcourse I do," Sattu said. "I practice what I preach."

"So you believe in God?" Vivek wondered.

"Let's say that I believe in the concept of God," Sattu clarified. Vivek looked confused.

"Yes, God is a concept, an ideology, invented by human beings when they got into existence. Some form of power, probably the purest form of power, which they can refer to whenever they need to."

Vivek continued. "So you think God didn't create human beings; instead human beings created Gods?"

"I know where you are coming from and we can debate on this all day. It's the classic chicken and egg situation, but the main point here is not who came first, but how we perceive this superpower, this source of endless energy we refer to as nature or God."

"What do you talk to them about?" Aakash was curious.

Sattu looked at him. "About everything."

Aakash was surprised. "You go to the temples and talk to them?"

"You can talk to them anywhere, anytime you want," Sattu said with great confidence.

Jai was next. "So you don't go to the temples?"

"I do go to temples, but for me it's more of a community exercise. Something I do to enjoy the vibes of the place."

Jai had another doubt. "What if someone decides not to go to the temple?"

Sattu shrugged. "Don't go if you don't feel like it. I am sure you don't go against your will to a night club."

Jai and Vivek looked at Aakash and avoided answering the rhetorical question. They had been dragged to the night clubs several times by their enthusiastic buddy.

Aakash had another point to make. "Interesting stuff, Sattu, quite interesting I must say, but I am still confused about this whole talk to the Gods thing. I mean should it be a formal conversation like. 'Dear God…I am fucked…please help, yours truly' or can it be a more liberal conversation like 'Hey God…wass up dude…you fucked my life…fuck back at you, yours faithfully'?"

Sattu smiled. "Say whatever you want to say, whatever makes you happy, they are your friends, talk to them as friends. Just open up with them like the way you opened up with me."

"Great…and can I do it when I am drunk?" Aakash added.

Sattu wasn't irritated. "Knock yourself out! Talk to them while you are drinking. In fact, drink with them, eat whatever you feel like. Do anything. None of the old traditional world bullshit. Just remember it's not the Gods who get angry, it's us."

Aakash turned to Vivek. "How are you going to drink in front of them? Is it your drinking day today?"

"What's that?" Sattu asked.

Vivek glared at Aakash for mocking him.

"Oh come on, Vivek!" Aakash teased.

Sattu looked from one to the other wondering what was going on.

"Sorry Sattu, I try and follow a schedule for drinking and eating non-vegetarian food," Vivek explained.

"Is that a religious schedule?"

"In a way."

"So, it's more superstitious?" Sattu asked.

Vivek squirmed. "I guess…"

"Well then, try and break it today!" Sattu said.

•

The day's assignment got them so excited that they rushed to the market to buy images and statues of Gods before going home. Even though Aakash insisted that they already had many images of Gods back home in the small little temple maintained by Vivek in his room, yet both Jai and Vivek were adamant that they should do the exercise in separate rooms, in privacy.

Aakash abided by Sattu's liberal opinion and opened a bottle of scotch and ordered some chicken. He spread the various images on the sofa and sat on the opposite side on the floor resting his back on the settee. As he gazed at the images, he found himself feeling sad at their serious expressions. He tried to start the conversation a couple of times by saying 'Hi' but did not know what to say next. So he decided to get drunk, hoping that the liquor would improve his conversational skills, like it always did in case of girls.

Jai, on the other hand, spread his set of images on the bed and looked at them consciously. His eyes travelled from Ganesha to Shiv to Parvati, from Raam to Sita, from Guru Nanak to Jesus, from Hanuman to Krishna and then back to Ganesha again. He kept looking at different images of Gods until he could hear the pounding in his heart.

Jai spoke with emotion. "Hello! Namaskar. You already know my name and everything about me. You even know what is there in my heart. I feel there is nothing new that I can tell you, but I don't know why after listening to Sattu, I have this urge to talk to you. You know me, I have always been confused. Earlier I used to feel guilty about it, but Sattu says it's good to be confused. It means that you are still alive, and I believe in Sattu. He is the Guru I never had. So, when he said that we should talk, I felt why not! I believe that my confusions have also been provided by you and no matter how confused I had been, you created a path for me – www.ihafa.in was not mine but your idea, and I somehow feel that even if it has not worked out today, you must be working out something better. I cannot tell you how light I feel after putting it all on your shoulders. Thank you for your attention!"

In his room, Vivek had gone into meditative mode. He practiced several forms of yoga to relax his brain and once he felt that he was in a position to talk, he gazed at the images and started.

"Pranam, I want to start by thanking you for giving me an extraordinary brain that I remained an achiever in my professional life, though I don't know if I should blame you for not giving me a normal heart. It seems the extra ounce of my brain you gave me was taken from my heart. In the last two years I have wandered enough, different gurus gave me different perspectives, but this is the first time someone asked me to talk to you. I am your creation, so where else can I go for any rectification. As I look back towards my life, there is only one thing that I ask, to give me some more heart so that I may get some more clarity. Pranam."

Aakash by now had finished half the bottle of scotch. The images were unclear to his eyes, but he had a comparatively clearer mind. He started.

"So Ganesha…wass up man? Even with your elephant head and big belly, you are quite popular," he said and winked.

"Any guy starts anything new, you are the God to go to, and you make it to all the marriage cards. I mean, that's commendable."

He gazed at Shiva, "And look at your dad, the God of moksha, nobody can escape him. He is in charge of heaven and hell; not to forget he is also the God who can get a girl married if she fasts on Mondays. I mean between the father-son duo, you guys cover a lot of followers in this country."

Aakash turned to Raam, "Still a rockstar around Diwali, nice going!"

Aakash grinned at Krishna, "But for me, you are my man – the God with the gopis and the Geeta." He winked. "I mean tell me, if it's all about karma, why did we get screwed? If you did this to us so that we can learn something out of it, then let me tell you that you are not such a good teacher."

He gulped a large amount of scotch straight from the bottle and glanced at Krishna for a response. But Krishna seemed oblivious to his sob story. He continued smiling, playing the bansuri and looking mystical. Aakash finally lost his patience and shouted out for his friends.

"You fuckers, come here! We have been fooled!"

Jai and Vivek hurried to the living room.

"Guys, Sattu lied. These Gods don't give answers."

They noticed the scotch bottle which was almost empty. It had hardly been an hour since they got home.

Vivek stared at him. "Aakash, you are drunk."

"So what? Sattu told me that I can get drunk...God does not mind."

"Exactly...it's not the God who minds, it's you."

"Don't fool me, do you have the guts to drink before Gods?"

"Yeah, why not?"

Aakash offered him his scotch bottle. Vivek took it with reluctance and made a peg for himself.

"Are you really going to drink?" Jai asked.

Vivek sat down quietly next to Aakash. "There is nothing wrong in drinking and there is nothing to feel guilty about. The Gods are my friends and I take this friendship forward by drinking to them."

He took a small sip glancing at the images.

Aakash slapped him on his back. "That's my man..."

He turned to Jai. "You too make a peg."

"I don't want to. I had a lot last night," Jai replied sternly.

Aakash shouted. *"Phattu saale...phat gayi bhagwaan se?"*

"I am not a phattu."

"Yes you are. I know your capacity, you haven't made them your friends yet!" Aakash teased.

Jai noticed Vivek was taking his second and a much bigger sip. He indicated that Jai should join them. Jai was wrought with guilt, yet he took a deep breath and made a drink for himself. He paused.

"Come on...what are you waiting for? Drink up."

Jai looked at Vivek who gestured him to go ahead. He reluctantly took a small sip.

"That's my boy...let the party begin...the God party."

They drank in silence for sometime. The idea of drinking before the Gods had still not sunk in completely. Not even for Aakash. For him, it was a gesture to rebel against his parents, against his childhood, against the unnecessary lectures and against the Gods who he blamed to have created all of this. He kept drinking and reached a point where he could only blabber.

"I knew it…I just knew it. Even if we make them our friends, they won't make friends with us. That's how the master-servant thing goes. The master may listen to his servant at times but friendship…nope, not at all. Look at them – just dumb like statues. How can such Gods control the entire world? You need some sort of smartness. But tonight, I won't let them have their way. I demand answers."

Jai smiled. "It's not night, it's still afternoon."

Jai's rectification triggered him further and he finally blasted out. "Whatever! I won't let them leave without an answer…They have to answer why they did what they did to us?"

He began to sob.

"Why did you give me such a father who kept bullshitting about the country's development, but made sure that he developed more than the country? Why did you give me a mother who patted me with appreciation only when I said something smart in her stupid parties? And why did you make me a person who waits for people to die before he can start loving them?"

His sobbing grew louder and his friends held him. They helped him on the bed and he fell asleep mumbling.

I had the Best Tea Ever

The next morning, Jai and Vivek woke Aakash up for breakfast. He sat up on the bed looking sheepishly at his friends. His eyes were swollen and his voice still heavy.

"Thanks man," he croaked.

Vivek patted him on the shoulder. "Thank your young bro. He made it."

"Thank you. It was quite a day yesterday...," Aakash said to Jai.

"Yours was best...you really opened up," Vivek said.

Aakash chewed slowly. "Did I cry a lot?"

"I don't know whether it qualifies as crying," Jai said sipping his chai. "You cried a lot but I could see only two drops of tears in your eyes."

Aakash sniffed. "That's how I cry man. My eyes are constipated. Listen, I was just thinking we should stop this module thing now."

Vivek shook his head. "Hey, it's not heavy if you try to surrender."

Aakash stared at him. "Have you surrendered?"

"I am trying...sincerely trying." Vivek said, leaning against the window.

The door bell rang, surprising them all. No one visited them in the morning. Jai ran out to open it. It was Nakul. He was on his way to office when he decided to check on his friends. He sauntered in and saw Aakash in bed.

"Hey Nakul...what a pleasant surprise!" Aakash said.

"What happened to your eyes?" Nakul asked, taking in the surroundings.

Aakash, recovering his strength and his sense of humour, smiled. "These guys beat me up yesterday...they said I need to surrender."

"Surrender to what?"

"To everything."

Vivek noticed Nakul's bland expression and changed the subject. "So you all set to go to the office?"

"Yeah. I thought I would just stop by and give you the bad news myself."

"What happened? Our investors decided to loot your bank and blame it on us?" Aakash asked.

Nakul shook his head. "No... but your investors have decided to loot your current account. They have blocked withdrawals from it."

Vivek shrugged. "That's expected. I'm not surprised."

Nakul was shocked. "What are they saying now?"

"They want us to take over their share and only then we can continue with the website."

"And how much are they asking for their share?"

Aakash continued with his breakfast. "We are still waiting for their price."

"No, they sent a mail this morning," Vivek said.

Aakash stopped chewing. "They did?"

"They are demanding three crores for their share."

Aakash banged the tray on the table. "Three fucking crores! Those bastards want to encash our vulnerability."

Jai took away the plates and cups, afraid Aakash may smash them in anger.

"Calm down. Let's discuss this with Sattu today in our meeting."

●

They returned to Sattu and his den which had now become their comfort zone. It seemed like a place where they could talk about anything. The presence of the books comforted them. It was like being surrounded by the wisdom of people from all over the world and a place where their insecurities and actions were not judged.

Sattu welcomed them and started their session for today. "So, how did it go?"

Jai was happy. "Satisfactory…I revealed everything to God and felt relieved."

Vivek agreed. "I felt there is some superpower that is going to take care of me."

Sattu turned to Aakash. "Did you talk to the Gods?"

"He talked a lot," Jai snickered.

Aakash glared at Jai.

Sattu continued. "Did you get any response, Aakash?"

Aakash remained silent, which was fine because Sattu had already noticed his swollen eyes.

"Who amongst you cried while talking to the Gods?"

Jai and Vivek looked at Aakash.

Sattu nodded. "Your crying is nothing but God's response to you."

Aakash looked at him sharply. "My crying was not God's response… it was my frustration."

Sattu leaned against the bookshelf. "But you have been frustrated for a while. How many times did you cry?"

Aakash had the answer, but decided not to say anything; this was not the first time that he had cried like that.

Sattu smiled. "One piece of good news for all of you. The toughest part of the module is over. Now it's just easy-peasy."

"You said the same thing yesterday!" Aakash said scornfully.

"No really. Today's assignment is actually easy."

"Before we go on to today's assignment, I wanted to share some news. The investors have asked us to cough up three crores for their share," Aakash said.

"I know. There's nothing new, that's how it starts. Then you do your calculations and make a counter offer, and then you sit down and negotiate, but we will come to that later, after the module is over. So, like I was saying, the previous assignments were about your truth. The next one is about the world's perception of your truth."

Sattu explained that entrepreneurship and IHAFA were their truths, but the world's perception of their truth was an essential point. How does the world perceive IHAFA? Was it a respectable platform or a cheesy one? Did this platform have well-wishers or were there more haters completely put off by it?

"We have had our share of hate mails and law suits," Vivek agreed with him.

"But that's part of every business," Aakash added.

"Try and meet some of them and listen to what they have to say about your platform," Sattu suggested.

"But they might get aggressive with us," Jai said worried.

"Don't be scared to confront them. Try to understand their point of view."

"So, we should go and meet our haters?" Aakash asked.

"You should go and meet the people who have been impacted by your platform."

The trio left his house and thought of people they should meet. Some of the people had sent them mails criticizing them of propagating negativity. One of them was the girl who was made fun of by her two office colleagues – Vinay and Vikram. Her name was Mandeep Kohli and her image was shattered in the office, so much so that she had to leave her job. Everybody in the office knew whom Vinay and Vikram had referred to in their video.

But, Mandeep did not sit quiet. She had sent a scalding mail to the IHAFA team and had even initiated a law suit for her supposed defamation.

They decided to start with meeting Mandeep and listen to her point of view. They found her number from the email and called her. Vivek was the one who heard her complain. Mandeep hardly let him speak as she vented her bitterness. But after a lot of persuasion, Vivek managed to get her to agree to a meeting. She chose a coffee shop. The three friends arrived at the designated time. When they saw Mandeep, it was clear that having her around in any office would be a huge distraction for any guy. Her beauty and personality were magnetic. Even though they had never met before, they instantly recognized that she was the one. They slowly entered the coffee place and greeted her politely.

Mandeep appeared upset and angry, but her fury made her look even hotter. This was going to be a tough test for them.

"We are really sorry for the embarrassment caused to you," Aakash began.

"No, you are not." Mandeep snapped. "Tell me something. What is it about a woman wearing a backless blouse that people get so excited?" She turned around to reveal her back and then continued. "Let's talk when you are done gaping."

They looked at each other sheepishly. Other people sitting in the coffee shop stared at this interesting group.

With bated breath, Vivek requested her to face them, and she did. "We had no idea that a video can have such repercussions," he said diplomatically.

"No wonder you have no idea about the painful effect it would have on anyone, or else you wouldn't have done the video which got you in jail," Mandeep replied coldly.

They were silenced by the memories of their own bitter experiences, and they sat with gloomy faces. She started feeling guilty. "Listen, I am sorry. But it's important for you to understand that other people can also get hurt in your growth process."

"We understand," replied Vivek and there was nothing more to say. There was an uncomfortable silence. They finally apologized again and took her leave.

She had touched a raw nerve. Even though they had started to realize the strong side effects of their platform, they decided to meet some more people to swallow the bitter pill. They were going through the list of hate mails and law suits when Sattu sent them a name – Rishiraj Sahay.

Rishiraj Sahay was a constable in the Delhi Police who was kicked out of the service because of negligence and inaction. The six-year-old daughter of a businessman had been killed in an accident and the culprits had escaped. When the police could not find them, an NGO worker recorded a video and raised issues about police inefficiency on IHAFA platform. The video went viral and police needed to take some action. They could only think of putting the blame on the constable who had taken a quick nap in his night jeep and missed the control room's message.

Before they went to meet Constable Rishiraj, Sattu told them some recently discovered facts. Constable Rishiraj had spent more than thirty hours as the guard of a senior politician, and was put on duty after that without a break. It was inhuman on the part of his department to make him work continuously. After suspending him, his senior told him that they had no option. The IHAFA platform had taken cognizance of the situation and made sure that they kept sharing the same video. Their intent was to push the police to take some action, but it had led to Rishiraj becoming the scapegoat. The best action that Rishiraj could have taken was to file a law suit against, IHAFA which he did promptly.

They decided to go visit the constable at his house without informing him. They reached the area where he lived with his family and parked their car. The narrow and winding lanes left them with no option but to go on foot. They walked through the stinking, dirty alleyways. It took them a while and after asking directions from several strangers, they located the kachcha makaan of Rishiraj. Two kids, probably his sons were playing outside with a small balboo stick and a tubeless tyre. Vivek asked the kids about their father. The kids called out to their mother. The lady with the *pallu* drawn over her head came out shyly and asked them about their purpose. Vivek went ahead and introduced them as the owners of the platform where the news spread. As if a storm had burst, she removed her pallu and gave them the choicest abuses, and slapped them. They initially tried to stop her, but she wept with such emotional pain that they accepted her vent without any resistance. Rishiraj noticed the commotion. He hurried outside, calmed his wife and led her inside. They noticed that the ex-constable was in a shabby state. Dressed in an unwashed shirt and trousers, he was a pitiful sight.

They introduced themselves. He didn't react and said. "It is better if you leave now."

"We are very sorry about what had happened," Vivek said with genuine concern. Unknowingly or otherwise, they had brought down a family from having a decent living to poverty. They expected Rishiraj to abuse them, but instead he looked at them calmly.

"It is not your fault. It is the nature of the service, and one or the other news channel would have picked up the issue and created a ruckus about it. It was just destined to happen."

"Can we help you in anyway?" they offered, feeling terribly guilty.

He shook his head and returned to his dilapidated home. The three were quite shaken as they gazed at the sad house before they turned away and made their way back to the car. Rishiraj's depressed demeanor and the thin kids affected them deeply and they drove home in silence. The incidents had shown them the dark side of their website. Sattu was right when he asked them to find out how society perceived their truth. On the way, they happened to pass under the same flyover where they had found their initial video contributor – the Man on the Street. Aakash could not help but notice small bathrooms built on one side of the flyover. He pointed them out to his friends and they parked the car to check them out.

They arrived to find the same family living there and the same kids begging. The man and his wife recognized them immediately and greeted them. Aakash queried about their well-being.

"Bahut badiya." The man replied and told them that within a few months, the video spread so much that the munincipal authorities had to construct bathrooms for all the families. They exchanged glances, never

expecting their website to bring about change at the grassroot level. A first positive effect. Vivek looked around. *"Ye to bahut achchi khabar hai… TV nahi lagaya gaya aapke liye?"*

The man shook his head and smiled sheepishly. *"Vo to hum bas bakchodi kar diye the, abhi ke liye to gusalkhaana hi kaafi hai."*

They shook hands with the man to say goodbye, but he wouldn't let them go. He gestured to his wife and she brought some tea in small glasses. It was a special treat just for them – a rare honour and respect for their guests. The three drank the best tea ever. Feeling overwhelmed with their generosity, they gave a few hundred rupees to the children. They returned home feeling at peace.

At home, they discussed the real impact of their platform. They admitted that they had wronged many people and probably helped many more as well. More than anything else, they were overwhelmed with their experiences. Meeting the people who had been adversely affected had opened their eyes and the one who had benefited from their efforts had made them feel better.

They started thinking on lines of how their platform could benefit people at large. But how would they get the platform back and even if so, how would they get it up and running without causing a stir?

The Roots – Mithai, Scotch and Adrak Chai

Back at the den, Sattu told Aakash, Jai and Vivek that there was only one last step required in the Clarity module – Going back to their roots.

"To what roots?" Aakash asked trying to show that he didn't understand it, even though he fully understood what Sattu meant.

Sattu didn't tell them anything much. He said that they would figure it out once they went there.

Jai headed to his hometown Saharanpur to meet his parents, visiting them after six months which was the longest he had ever been away. They welcomed him with open arms. The business and the political aftermath, the media coverage and his nights at jail led them to assume that Jai was depressed.

For the first two days, Jai did nothing but relax. But there was one activity he could not switch off, and that was his brain. It ticked non-stop, revisiting so many different aspects of his life. He was nostalgic about small-town life. A bowl of rajma would arrive from a neighbour just because it was delicious and had to be shared. People would barge into the neighbour's house unannounced to gossip, or share some tidbits. It was a kind of neighbourhood where an uncle willingly parked his scooter in the middle of the road so that children could make a wicket on its stepney and play cricket.

Then one day when he was sitting in their family-owned sweet shop, a casual conversation with his parents transformed their relationship forever.

His mother turned to him, holding a piece of mithai. *"Ye le, ye try kar."*

Jai looked at it. *"Kya hai?"*

She stuffed it into his mouth. *"Kaju-badam mix barfi...bahut chal rahi hai ye aaj kal."*

Jai chewed slowly and enjoyed it.

His father was at the cash register. He glanced up and said. *"Isko paan laddoo khilayo."*

"Vo kya hai?" Jai asked, never heard that one in their traditional shop. They always had the regular stuff.

His mother gave him a paan laddoo. *"Khaa ke dekh...paan se bhi zyaada tasty hai."*

Jai tasted and found it surprisingly delicious. *"To aaj kal innovation chal raha hai."*

His father took off his spectacles. *"Vo kya hota hai?"*

Jai thought for a moment then said, "*Matlab* experiment"

His father smiled. *"Haan. Experiment chal rahe hain...abhi to asli cheez yahan pe hai hi nahin."*

"Achcha?" Jai wondered where his father was going with this conversation. There was always a purpose to his discussions. And the last time, his father had totally criticized his decision to leave his job and join his friends in a crazy undertaking.

"Chocolate *barfi do mahine pehle banayi thi...bahut bikee. Ab diwali pe layenge, aaj kal to* fashion *hai diwali pe* chocolates gift *karne ka."*

Jai was curious at this new turn. They never ventured outside the traditional recipes. *"Kis tarah ki chocolate barfi banayi thi?"*

Mother smiled proudly. *"Sab tarah ki – tumhaari* Dairy Milk, Five Star, Gems *aur vo kaun se laddoo aate hain?"*

Jai smiled. "Ferrero Rocher?"

"Haan wahi...vo bhi banayi thi."

Jai was impressed. *"Sahi ja rahe ho aap log!"*

"Jayenge hi, jab beta itna bada businessman ho to humein bhi to reputation rakhni padegi," his mother said proudly. Her comment struck a nerve, he nodded while he recalled the bitter experience with his business. His father decided to bring it up.

"Dekh beta…zindagi mein utaar-chadhaav to lage hi rahte hain. Ab is dukaan ko hi dekh lo. Chhe mahine pehle tak ye kuch khaas nahi chalti thi. Phir tumhe dekh kar humein bhi josh aaya. Socha kuch naya try karte hain. Aur ab sab badal gaya. Ab yahan paanch ladkon ki fauj hai hamare paas."

His father considered a team of five guys working for them as an army for such a small city.

Jai looked around the small store. It had faced ups and downs but thrived by his parents' sheer willpower and optimism.

"Himmat karo aur dobara shuruwaat karo." His father said giving him a pat on the back.

Jai was taken aback by their reaction. *"Main to sochta tha ki aap log mujhe phir naukri ke liye bolenge."*

Mother shook her head. *"Na beta na…tu naukri nahi karega ye to main tere bachpan se hi samajh gayi thi jab baaki bachche cricket khelte the aur tu comics ka stall laga ke unhe kiraye pe deta tha."*

"To matlab aap log naaraz nahi ho?" Jai asked.

Father smiled. *"Naaraz kis liye beta, tune itna bada kaam kiya. Logon ko awaaz di, phir bhi tujhe sorry bolna hai to bol de, hum to maan-baap hain…maaf kar hi denge."*

He stared at his parents with newfound respect. They hugged each other with a renewed sense of bonding.

Jai leaned away. *"To mujhe ab kya karna chahiye?"*

"Waapis jayo usi avaam ke paas jinko tumne awaaz di thi…aur unse kaho ki mujhe meri awaaz waapis chahiye." His father declared.

Jai was so happy with their support. *"Ye to humein sujha hi nahi."*

His father smiled. *"Kuch cheezein tajurbe ke saath aati hain,"* he said as he opened one of the boxes.

"Lekin hamare investors ke paas to bahut tajurba hai."

"Kuch cheezein laalach ke saath chali bhi jaati hain," he said.

Jai thought about it. *"Lekin vo paise jo main har mahine bhejta tha?"*

His mother pitched in. *"Dukaan achchi chal rahi hai Puttar...ab uski zaroorat nahi hai."*

She took out another piece of the sweet from the box and fed him.

"Le...mun meetha karle."

•

Aakash visited his father at his Lucknow residence. They were meeting after a gap of two years. Like thorough gentlemen, they shook hands firmly. His father asked him to join him at his various commitments. Initially Aakash was reluctant, but thought to himself that he may as well interact with his father, who seemed like a stranger.

They started the day with the inauguration of a computer laboratory at a government school where his father was the chief guest. He made a speech on the importance of education and the role of computers in this changing world. They then proceeded to a government hospital which had recently started free medical check-up mobile vans in the rural areas. His father, again the chief guest, made another speech about the importance of medical facilities in rural areas. They attended several such events. At all these meets, his father introduced Aakash as the Founder of www.ihafa.in. This surprised Aakash. Besides, when Aakash had mentioned his venture and his partnership with his friends, his father had not only discouraged but had also criticized him. Aakash was surprised when almost every businessman greeted him like a celebrity and appreciated his business idea. They even empathized with him on the sudden closure of the website due to political interference. His father could not hide his smile of pride. Aakash could not help but feel happy that his father was acknowledging him as an intelligent adult.

As he spent the day with him, he noticed two qualities which he had never noticed earlier – his father was an excellent orator and he had solutions for some of the problems faced by people in their daily lives. They arrived home in the evening and Aakash joined his father for a drink in the drawing room. His father gave him the unopened bottle of scotch. "Do you remember this?"

Aakash shook his head.

"This is the same vintage scotch you sent me as a gift."

"You haven't opened it yet?"

His father smiled. "I was waiting for a special occasion and here we are are today."

He poured generous pegs into two glasses. They sipped the single malt. They were silent for a few moments. Aakash noticed his father; he looked exhausted and old.

"So what's new?"

"Nothing much…feel kind of blank about the next move," Aakash confessed.

His father added a cube of ice in his drink. "But you look fairly happy."

Aakash smirked. "Yeah! Probably because of this Clarity module I am attending with my friends."

"Clarity module?" His father asked.

"Yeah. It's about self discovery."

His father gazed at the golden liquid in his glass. "Sounds interesting. Your mother and I attended such a workshop together. Our marriage was not working out and we had already tried the second and third honeymoons, so we went for a couples' workshop."

Aakash didn't know about the strain in their relationship. "How was it?"

"Bloody good. Our marriage never faltered after that."

"What exactly changed after the workshop?" Aakash had never heard his father admit any fault or any weaknesses.

"Well, we started giving space to each other. That kind of worked well for the both of us. We followed the same in your upbringing, but it seems that kids do not need space…its only the adults who need it."

Aakash smiled. "I guess so…you gave me too much space."

His father finished his drink and made another. "I couldn't help it son, they give huge homes to IAS officers."

Aakash sipped his drink, hesitated and then spoke up. "Do you miss Mom?"

His father was staring at his glass, lost in his own world. Aakash noticed the fleeting expressions of regret and sadness.

"These scotch glasses were bought by your mother on our tenth anniversary. Every Saturday, we would get together for a couple of drinks and bitch about people. That was our 'me time'. You know alcohol has this quality of bringing people together. We really opened up to each other when we got drunk."

"Then why did you ask me to slow down? Everytime you told me to slow down, I used to think how should I tell my dad that Dad when you drink, you get drunk but when I drink I feel awakened!"

He laughed. "I bet every guy wants to say the same thing to his dad, but I asked you to slow down because you were going too fast. Even your mom used to worry about your drinking habits."

"So you do miss her?"

His father smiled and gestured for bottoms up. He did not need to answer his question; it was obvious.

"Change your website a bit," his father said, while he made another round of drinks for them.

He handed Aakash his glass. "Change it how?"

"Give it a positive angle. Your idea is good but it currently gives a negative vibe. It has that irritating feel, like one of those sleazy news channels always cribbing and trying to create sensational news. When you create a business on negativity, how can you avoid feeling the wrath someday?"

That was deep, Aakash realized. His father was damn wise.

"What should we do about it, Dad?"

"Ask people to also share some good experiences, some positive interactions, some achievements after a long struggle. Life is not always bad."

"That's a valid point. But we can't do anything yet, the site is completely blocked."

"If you want, I can try and cool down the bastard. I can talk to him through some of my friends in Delhi."

"I don't think that would be required."

"I know that. You are a smart guy. You will work something out."

Aakash was flabbergasted; his father never had a positive word for him. And here he was being a...a dad.

His father looked at him with gentleness. "I hope you don't hate me anymore."

Aakash was taken aback. "Why would I do that?"

"We never really spoke like this. We should also get together every Saturday. Make this a habit."

Aakash grinned. "Of course, Dad! Although once a month would be possible."

"That sounds good. So you don't hate me anymore." His father made an emotional eye contact. They remained with each other for a while.

"How can I hate you? You are my father!" And with those words Aakash felt the huge weight of resentment fade away. Father and son shared an awkward hug, and that night Aakash slept like a baby.

•

Vivek managed to get one more meeting with Aarti. He was surprised when she answered his call and agreed. After their divorce, he thought she would have deleted his number. He invited her to a coffee shop but she asked him to come home.

At her home, Vivek was quite amused to see Aarti in a sari and serving him his favourite adrak chai with samosas. Aarti appeared nervous, she was twisting the edge of her sari around her fingers but decided to break the ice. "I thought of messaging you, you know when all this happened. But then I thought you may get angry, so I checked with your parents."

Vivek savoured the chai. "I would have liked it if you had called."

"I don't know…you had just signed the divorce papers around that time."

"Yeah that's true, life was just so hectic." He nibbled on a samosa.

Aarti nodded sympathetically. "I guess a lot has happened in a short span of time."

Vivek was enjoying the soft side of Aarti. "You know, my life has been like that guy who goes through years to prove he is worthy. Of what, I don't know. But basically success was the motto, and failure was considered a bad word. There was no room for failure in anything I did. I think that attitude caused me to be this way."

There was an awkward silence. Vivek finished his tea. "So you are seeing anyone?" He dared to ask.

Aarti nodded. "Yes, we just started meeting. It's an arranged set-up."

Vivek felt a twang of disappointment. "Good for you…All the best!" he said brightly.

Aarti was surprised at his response. "Thanks. Any special reason you wanted to meet?"

"Actually yes. Aarti, I didn't want to end all of this the way it ended. In fact, I didn't want to end it at all, but that's okay. I just came here to apologize for all my insecurities and to thank you for being a fantastic support."

Aarti smiled, looking relieved. "Thanks! You are a good person Vivek. But, sometimes things don't always work out the way you expect."

Vivek grinned. "That's true."

"I really liked your website. I felt like using it."

"Thank God you didn't use my own platform to vent out against me!" Vivek said lightly.

"I mean people want to be heard, although I would have really enjoyed if it had the option of asking questions and getting an answer."

"You mean like a counseling platform?" He started on another samosa.

"Exactly!"

"That's amazing. I think we should try and do that once we get the platform back."

How did we get Screwed?

With purpose and renewed optimism, Vivek, Aakash and Jai went to Sattu's house unannounced. Their agenda was clear – they needed to do one more recording.

Sattu entered the room and did not indicate even a fraction of surprise on seeing them. He seemed to know that once they returned from their roots, they would have gained clarity.

Aakash was enthusiastic. "We have decided to record one more video."

"A collective video," Vivek added.

"Where we ask for people's support to get our website back!" Jai said.

Sattu nodded. "And then?"

Aakash smiled. "And then upload it on social media."

"Yes, spread the buzz of our eagerness to return."

"We expect it will have an impact," Jai joined in.

"And what about the investors?"

"Let's hope it spreads so well that Rajendra Yadav can take back his decision of not letting the website run!" Aakash said with a wave.

"That's quite optimistic," Sattu said calmly.

"I am sure the media will help spread the story…they keep trying to reach us for our future plans," Aakash said.

Sattu was serious. "What if the investors still don't agree?"

"We will keep pushing them," Jai offered.

Sattu was not as enthusiastic. "So you guys have already decided."

They chorused an eager yes.

Sattu looked grim. "And you are not going to go back on this?"

They shook their heads and announced a 'no' in a strong voice.

"Okay. Where do you want to do it? In my reading room or on the terrace?"

"Reading room!" they chorused.

"You all seem to be in sync today?"

"Yes!" they chorused again.

"Have you also decided on what you are going to say?"

"We will just speak from our hearts," Aakash said.

"Really? An impromptu thing?"

Vivek giggled. "No, he is just screwing with you, we have it memorized."

"Great! Screw the man who showed you why the screwing happens!" Sattu laughed sarcastically.

In the reading room, Sattu had the camera propped up and ready while the trio took ten minutes to get ready for the video. Sattu was amused when they appeared. They were wearing some chunky jewellery, rings and heavy chains. They even carried some hawan samagri with them. Vivek had gone all out and wore a saffron t-shirt with OM printed on it. He held mala-beads in his hands.

The trio stood together in the frame, faced the camera and started speaking.

"Hi! We are all here to talk to you about something important," Vivek started.

"Please don't worry. We are not here to sell these rings and chains," Jai added lightly.

"But we definitely want to talk about them." Aakash clasped his hands together and nodded like a sadhu.

"Yes definitely. I have invested a lot of time in my life trying to understand what's going to happen and that too through our favourite means – astrology," Vivek added.

"Does it include The Big Bang?" Jai asked, turning to his friend.

"Well, I don't know about that, but it definitely relates to planetary movements and their impact."

"So what do the rings do?" Aakash asked.

"The rings manipulate the impact," Vivek replied. Jai and Aakash exchanged puzzled looks.

"Let me explain. This ring is to lure Rahu. This one is for Ketu. This is Moti which is meant to keep you calm. This one is Pukhraj for prosperity. This bead is for concentration and this chain is to protect you from evil," Vivek summed up as he showed his rings and chains.

"You are so sorted out, Vivek. I also wear this ring because I am a Manglik and this chain due to my sadhe-sati," Jai added.

"But if your sadhe-sati is going on, then no ring can save you!"

"What are you saying?" Jai asked terrified.

"He is right. It basically means that you are screwed for seven-and-a-half years, buddy," Aakash said.

"Seven-and-a-half years? My astrologer told me that I will have three such rotations of sadhe-sati. It means my working life is fucked," Jai said hopelessly.

"Don't worry. I have a solution for that." Vivek pacified him and pulled up a hawan kund. "This hawan is going to get rid of all those bad luck sadhe-satis."

"Oh really! All my fucked up stars will start behaving properly?"

"Not only that. You can also get rid of any vices you did in your past lives, cleansing your past karmas," Vivek replied.

"Really man! If that's the case then why did your marriage fail and get screwed up?" Aakash snapped.

"I think we should start with the basics – the Big Bang," Jai covered up.

"Leave the fucking Big Bang. Let's talk about today: We the educated smart youth of this country, I mean why do we do what we do?"

"Because it seems the right thing to do," Jai replied.

"Social influences," Vivek replied.

"Do you mean to say that we do not have a thinking brain and we all follow blindly?" Jai asked naively.

"We have brains but we hardly use them," Vivek replied.

"It means we are clones of each other?"

"Yeah. Social cloning started much before DNA cloning."

"What does that mean?"

"It means we react more than we act," Aakash replied.

"What's wrong with that?"

"Who said it's about right or wrong? It's just the way we are."

"If we are clones of each other, why do we have different nationalities?"

Vivek nudged him. "You idiot! If we don't have different addresses, how will I send you a courier?"

Jai slapped his forehead, "Oh right!"

Aakash pitched in. "But the internet does not ask for my nationality, it just asks the name and whoa! There you are."

"Well, it does ask for nationalities and addresses. How do you think our office was shut down?"

Jai felt low and said, "One morning a girl came crying to us claiming that she was raped by none other than the honorable MLA Rajendra Yadav."

Vivek nodded. "Her clothes were torn, her body hurt. We had no way to figure out that she was lying and we offered our support and our sympathetic shoulders."

Aakash looked glum. "We cried with her, but she ditched us. But we were not the only ones to weep with her. The whole nation cried with her." He raised his hands in the air.

Jai snapped. "Was it genuine crying or just social influences?"

Vivek looked straight at the camera "We gave you a platform."

Aakash was loud, "A place where the man on the street unloads his problem and finds a resolution."

Jai had a firm expression. "Yes...where a eunuch scholar spoke about her helpless parents."

"But this platform was shut down."

"It was taken away from us."

"It was taken away from *you*."

"But we won't stoop or falter anymore. We will not wear these rings of diplomacy or these chains of guilt," Vivek added as the three of them took off all the rings and chains and flung them aside.

"Neither will we do any hawan of apology," Aakash added.

"We will just stand here for two minutes in silence, not because a platform was shut, but because a spirit was killed," Jai concluded.

The three friends then stood there for two minutes with their heads bowed. When the video ended Sattu choked and clapped. He hugged them for their earnest attempt.

"I think we should upload this video now," Vivek said.

"Not now, but soon enough," Sattu said eagerly.

"But why not now?" Vivek asked.

"First you need to buy back the website from your investors."

Show me the Money

Sattu's advice of finding money to buy back their share gave them renewed confidence to search for more investors. They spent days trying to think about whom they could ask the money from. It was a dilemma – Sattu's logic was that if they bought the investor's share, they would get a huge bargain. Once the videos were uploaded and if they became viral, then the investors might ask for a higher price or may even want to own it. But, after going through what had happened, the trio was clear that they did not want to continue with the same investors. It was a catch-22 situation. Until they uploaded the videos, their chances of finding an investor were dismal. They decided to approach some others, but mostly got a cold response.

Aakash thought of borrowing money from his father. After their quality time together, he would want to do something for his son.

While they were contemplating the situation, Vivek received a call from Sahitya. They had another benefactor – Ramakant Chaturvedi. The video uploaded for the archaeologist had earned him a healthy budget from an international NGO for his silver jubilee excavation in resurrection of monuments and cultural heritages. And he had promised that if he received any benefit as a result of IHAFA platform, he would offer them a gift. Ramakant fulfilled his promise. At a recent auction, he sold one of his precious artifacts and presented the trio with a generous cheque.

Vivek asked Sattu to start negotiations with the investors for their share of business. The negotiations were carried out well and continued for a couple of weeks until finally the investors arrived at an amount of 2.17 crores. Even though Vivek could not figure out how investors calculated the abstract figure, the three friends decided not to debate on it further.

They gathered in the same room facing the same group of people who had fired them. Sattu wanted to avoid any kind of ill-feelings and stayed away from the meetings and preferred to remain in the background, preparing them on the art of negotiation. Both the parties signed their papers finally and shook hands on the deal. But before they exited the room, the fund director was curious.

"So, you managed to find an investor. But, how do you plan to calm down the politician?"

Aakash smiled. "We don't have any plan for the politician. And we didn't find an investor. Things just fell into place."

"How did things just fall into place?"

Jai smirked, "We just whispered to Ganpati and he got the money for us."

The fund committee looked at them in shock. Aakash, Vivek and Jai exited the room laughing heartily. Sattu finally uploaded all their videos and even before they could seek help from the media, the videos spread like wildfire. The founders of www.ihafa.in admitted to being Confused Bastards and asked for the platform to being returned to people. Debate started all over the country in various forums about returning the people's platform to the public. The trio regained their celebrity status with their confession label of Confused Bastards. Aakash's strong self-declaration about puberty and globalization also resulted in a huge female following. He could not thank Sattu enough for the love he received from those women.

The increased involvement by the media pressurised Rajendra Yadav's political party, who now felt that the platform was going to result in vote loss. They could not say anything negative against the resurgence of the IHAFA. As for the fund committee, they felt cheated that the videos had not been disclosed earlier. Sattu finally opened his cards and told them that they should have supported the founders right through their tough times rather than just shutting down the platform. He wanted them to realize that it was easy to talk about raw fresh energies, but it was more important to support and manage those energies.

"You can't win a match by taking the side of the winning team. Who would have anticipated such response for their videos?" he concluded.

The fund managers had no answer.

Their videos continued creating an uproar, especially among the youth. The culprits had now become the underdogs and everybody from media to social pundits who had earlier criticized their platform, came out supporting them. But the monster who had made their lives miserable still needed to be encountered.

They requested the secretary of Meera Juneja that they want to appear on her show. Meera was planning to host a "Q & A" session of Yadav in front of the people and allowed them to participate in the show. They sat amongst an audience of over a hundred people in the TV studio. Yadav was greeted with flowers and applause. The show started and the host started asking questions from Yadav. Questions ranging from water to electricity to roads were asked. Yadav rendered perfectly nuanced answers resulting in positive feedback from the people. Even the tough question regarding his association with Bhasha Raam Bapu, who was recently thrown in jail for running a sex racket, was answered by him with aplomb. "It was wrong judgment on my part. I was wrong about Bhasha Raam Bapu. I wish Shree Krishna gives me so much wisdom that I am able to judge between right and wrong people."

The whole show seemed orchestrated like a goodwill building exercise for Yadav. But Aakash, Jai and Vivek caught him on the wrong foot when Meera invited questions from the audience. Aakash raised his hand and received the mike. When he stood up, Yadav noticed him and his partners sitting in the crowd.

Before Aakash could speak, the host of the show introduced all the founders of www.ihafa.in. The crowd cheered. Many had recognized them earlier but the introductions triggered a huge round of applause for the trio, taking the entire focus of the show away from Yadav. He could not intimidate the host, but gave her an irate stare nonetheless. It didn't faze her.

Aakash opened with utmost humility. "Sir, it's very humbling to hear from an esteemed political leader that he was wrong in judging a crook in the disguise of a Sadhu. Very seldom we see people, especially at such senior levels admitting their failure of judgment." He took a pause before continuing. Jai and Vivek stood up to give him support. "Sir...we also failed that morning when that girl turned up at our office. She was in torn clothes, had brusies on her body and was a damn good actor, much more intense than Bhasha Raam Bapu."The crowd laughed at his wit.

"We got fooled and we paid the price. We spent two nights in prison and our platform was shut. But, we realized that we were wrong. We apologize to you sir that you suffered because of our lack of judgment."

If anybody could have looked at Yadav's face at the minutest level, they would have noticed that he looked like the biggest Confused Bastard ever. Angst spread across his face, but he could not express it. With all his desperation to get the big MP ticket for the upcoming elections, he finally uttered a few words for the eager audiences. "It's ok. It happens in life. Life is all about experiences."

Aakash, Jai and Vivek led the audience into a round of applause. The host smiled at Yadav. She knew Yadav's discomfort was not over. The trio immediately came up with another request.

"Sir, after a lot of struggle and negotiations, we have managed to get our platform back from our investors. We plan to make it online in a few days. The new platform won't just be for people cribbing, but also for people who have positive experiences. It is our request to you to please inaugurate this new platform."

Yadav squirmed uncomfortably. Accepting apology in a public forum was one thing, but to inaugurate the platform which ruined his image was something he could never accept. He politely stood up to turn down the offer. "I am happy that you have your platform back and you want me to come for the inauguration, but due to the upcoming elections, my schedule is very tight."

But the host cut him short. She encouraged him to participate. "Come on, Yadavji. You can manage fifteen minutes for the youth of this country. They will feel great."

Just when Yadav was about to come up with another excuse, Jai's active-only-in-last-moments-of-stress brain gave him an idea and he acted on it. He began chanting Yadav's name initially at a lower pitch, but as Vivek and other people joined him, the chorus got louder and louder. In a few moments, the whole crowd chorused and Yadav had no option but to oblige.

The eventful day arrived pretty fast. Yadav snipped the ribbon at the IHAFA head office and joined the entrepreneurs on a specially prepared stage while the media repeatedly took pictures and asked questions about Yadav supporting the platform. In the next few days, Yadav received positive reviews for forgiving and forgetting. He kept repeating the same four words in the press conferences: "Let bygones be bygones."

Epilogue

Aakash, Jai and Vivek invited Ramakant, Sahitya, Sheena, Nakul and Sneha for a small get together and Sattu was kind enough to host it at his house. They thanked Sattu, Ramakant and Sahitya for their timely guidance and support.

Jai apologized to Sheena for not taking her calls, but she didn't mind. She was eager to meet Sneha who was on her way to the party.

Ramakant sipped his scotch, staring at the Happy Gods on the walls and smiling constantly. "Nice idea!" he commented, appreciating Sattu's effort to depict the Gods in a lighter way.

Sahitya asked the trio, "What changes are you making to the website?"

"We have decided to change the name of the website. The full form has been changed from 'I have a Frustrated Ass' to 'I have a Fantastic Ass'. Now people can use this website to highlight good things about life, about society, and about each other," Jai explained.

Sattu smiled with appreciation. "So you guys are diversifying!"

Ramakant was impressed. "You helped them the right way, Sattu. They seemed to have learned fast."

"I just helped them to look deeper. They were stressed out, confused, but it's your help which got them the full share of their business, Ramakant."

Ramakant smiled sheepishly. "Well, that artifact was just gathering dust in my house," he helped himself to the various snacks.

"Don't you think you could have sponsored your own excavation with that money?" Sattu asked.

Ramakant sipped on is drink. "Oh no…not at all…that money is not adequate for my next and last excavation."

"But what you did for us is nothing less than a miracle, Ramakant sir," Vivek said with humility.

They heard footsteps hurrying towards the living room, and in popped a young woman.

Sattu welcomed her inside. "My daughter."

"Sneha?" Jai was shocked.

"You two know each other?" Sattu asked genuinely surprised.

Aakash and Vivek chorused. "Sneha is Sattu's daughter?!"

Sneha smiled nervously. "So, how is the party going?"

"You can't answer a question with a question," Sattu said.

Sneha laughed. "But everybody's asking questions, I thought I might as well join in."

"How do you know him?" Sattu demanded.

Jai and Sneha were behaving awkwardly, clearly embarrassed to admit their relationship.

Aakash took it upon himself to explain. "They are a couple."

Sattu stared wide-eyed. "A couple!"

Sneha patted her father's arm. "Relax Dad…I told you I am seeing someone."

"But you never told me his name!"

"What difference would that have made?" Sneha asked calmly. Jai was nervous at Sattu's reaction.

"It's not about the difference…it's just that…"

Aakash and Vivek viewed the scene.

Aakash whispered to Vivek. "Looks like Sattu can also become speechless."

Vivek whispered back. "He's reviewing the right response."

Aakash hissed. "Someone rightly said that answering your children is the best way God can ask you to shut the fuck up."

"I think this is God's sarcasm,"Vivek murmured.

Aakash giggled. "I have a new theory. The climax of sex is orgasm and the climax of satire is sarcasm."

Jai turned to Sneha. "And why didn't you tell me?"

Sneha laughed. "Oh come on...you are not the aggrieved party here."

Jai was embarrassed with her answer but quickly raised another relevant question. "But don't you live here?"

"I am an independent person."

Jai became red and he decided to stay out of it. Sneha took matters in her hands. She smiled. "Let me introduce both of you to each other. Dad, that's Jai. Jai, meet my Dad."

Both shook hands again with a strange awkwardness.

"I think you guys should hug each other," Sneha said.

A hug seemed too much to expect, but they obliged.

Ramakant stood up to pat Sattu. "The couple looks good together."

Sattu took a few moments to accept it. But he soon realized that he should be able to practice what he preached and accept change which was the only truth in life.

Sheena could not contain her excitement and started off with, "Oh! What a lovely couple. That's how Nakul and I used to be during our dating days. I wish I could get those days back."

"I hope not!" replied Nakul surprising himself more than anyone else. Sheena looked embarrassed but everyone laughed it off. Nakul gained confidence and asked the IHAFA founders, "So, what's next after the platform is up and running?"

Sattu looked at them for the answer. He already knew the answer but was curious enough to hear it. The trio smiled at each other as Aakash finally said the words, "*Silicon Valley*!"